PRISON PLANET

Starbuck leaned back against the metal bars of his cell. The door swung open with a raspy squeak.

"What the heck..." he said as he stumbled into the corridor.

"Get back inside," Assault called anxiously. "Close your door, mate."

"They don't like us to do that," said Adulteress, frowning through her bars at him.

"You mean that none of these cells are locked?"

"They haven't worked in generations," answered Assault.

Starbuck was dumbfounded. "Why the heck, if you don't mind my asking, do you stay here then?"

"Tradition," answered Forger.

Berkley Battlestar Galactica Books

BATTLESTAR GALACTICA
by Glen A. Larson and Robert Thurston

BATTLESTAR GALACTICA 2: THE CYLON DEATH MACHINE
by Glen A. Larson and Robert Thurston

BATTLESTAR GALACTICA 3: THE TOMBS OF KOBOL
by Glen A. Larson and Robert Thurston

BATTLESTAR GALACTICA 4: THE YOUNG WARRIORS
by Glen A. Larson and Robert Thurston

BATTLESTAR GALACTICA 5: GALACTICA DISCOVERS EARTH
by Glen A. Larson and Michael Resnick

BATTLESTAR GALACTICA 6: THE LIVING LEGEND
by Glen A. Larson and Nicholas Yermakov

BATTLESTAR GALACTICA 7: WAR OF THE GODS
by Glen A. Larson and Nicholas Yermakov

BATTLESTAR GALACTICA 8: GREETINGS FROM EARTH
by Glen A. Larson and Ron Goulart

BATTLESTAR GALACTICA 9: EXPERIMENT IN TERRA
by Glen A. Larson and Ron Goulart

BATTLESTAR GALACTICA 10: THE LONG PATROL
by Glen A. Larson and Ron Goulart

BattlestaR
GALACTICA 10
THE LONG PATROL

Novel by Glen A. Larson and Ron Goulart
Based on the Universal Television Series
"BATTLESTAR GALACTICA"
Created by Glen A. Larson
Adapted from the episode
"The Long Patrol"
Written by Donald Bellisario

BERKLEY BOOKS, NEW YORK

BATTLESTAR GALACTICA 10:
THE LONG PATROL

A Berkley Book/published by arrangement with
MCA PUBLISHING, a Division of MCA, Inc.

PRINTING HISTORY
Berkley edition/November 1984

ISBN: 0-425-07105-7

A BERKLEY BOOK ® TM 757,375
Berkley Books are published by The Berkley Publishing Group,
200 Madison Avenue, New York, N.Y. 10016.
The name "Berkley" and the stylized "B" with design
are trademarks belonging to Berkley Publishing Corporation.
PRINTED IN THE UNITED STATES OF AMERICA

CHAPTER ONE

Majestically the *Galactica* moved through the deep blackness of starless space. The gigantic, multi-level vehicle was the greatest fighting ship in the Colonial Fleet, a self-contained world housing thousands.

The person who oversaw the destiny of those thousands, and of the hundreds in the rest of the rag-tag fleet, was Commander Adama, a broad-shouldered, grey-haired man. He stood on the bridge of the battlestar and gazed out the large observation window into the intense darkness.

Colonel Tigh approached him. "The sensors indicate," he said, "that we're nearly through the asteroid dust."

"It's odd," said Adama as he turned away from the dark window. "I feel nervous, as uneasy as a cadet on his first orbit."

The boy who was standing beside the commander said, "I don't think I'm nervous. But maybe that's because I sort of don't know what's going on exactly."

Captain Apollo, the boy's father, stepped away from the data panel he'd been studying. Putting his hand on his son's shoulder, he said, "This is what's happening, Boxey. We've left our star system and, when we're through this field of asteroid dust, there'll be a whole new galaxy."

"A brand new place?"

"For us, yes. A galaxy nobody in our fleet has ever seen before."

"Commander," said Tigh, nodding at the wide view window, "we're through."

Stars were appearing in the silent blackness outside. A sparkle of light here, another there. Soon dozens, then hundreds. And then there were thousands of stars glowing in space, surrounding the *Galactica* and the fleet.

Boxey observed, "A heck of a lot of stars."

"And now that you've seen 'em, nipper," suggested Apollo as he tousled his son's hair, "you'd better turn in. You're already centons past your sleep period."

"Do I have to? I mean, we're in a new galaxy and all," said Boxey. "This is a terrific educational experi—"

"Bed."

The boy glanced toward his grandfather. "Shouldn't I maybe stay up?"

Assuming a relatively stern look, the commander told him, "I command the fleet, young fellow, but Apollo's your father."

Shoulders slumping, Boxey said, "Okay, I'll go to

bed and miss everything." He began a slow, forlorn exit from the bridge.

"Seems to me," said Apollo, watching him go, "that you and I used to have similar debates when I was about that age, Dad."

"You were usually more dramatic," said Adama, smiling. "Quite good at stamping your foot."

Colonel Tigh rejoined them. "Initial sensor readings are negative," he reported. "No indications of life forms within the first quadrant of this new galaxy."

"As soon as the rest of the fleet clears the asteroid dust," Adama said, "concentrate all the sensors forward to increase our scanning range."

"Yes, sir."

The commander, followed by Apollo, walked over to a console manned by the dark-haired Athena. "If we get a hint of anything out there, we'll have to send out a reconnaissance ship" he said. "And it'll be our new Recon Viper."

Apollo said, "We've already got a volunteer to pilot the new ship."

"Who?" inquired the commander.

"Lieutenant Starbuck," answered the captain, smiling faintly.

"Starbuck?" said the pretty Athena, sitting up. "I didn't know he ever volunteered for anything."

"He's got a strong sense of duty," Apollo assured her. "And besides, ever since the Council gave permission to the Scorpios to reopen the Astro Lounge over on the Edena, Starbuck's been trying to raise enough money to get into the place. Father's offered a hundred cubit flight bonus to the first pilot who flies our new Recon Viper."

"Don't deprecate his volunteering," said the commander. "Bonus or not, the mission may be a long and dangerous one."

"Far be it from me to suggest my old buddy's mercenary," said Apollo.

Adama nodded at Athena. "What's Starbuck's status at the moment?"

She touched a few of the buttons on her console panel. Names of warriors scrolled up the console's display screen. When Starbuck's came up, the crawl ceased.

Athena tapped the screen with her forefinger. "He's Status Green," she said. "Right now he's on the Rising Star."

Nodding, Commander Adama said, "Let's hope we don't have to jump him to Status Red until after his dinner." He moved on.

Athena touched Apollo's arm. "Starbuck asked me to dinner tonight," she said frowning. "But I wanted to be here when we sighted the new galaxy."

"Little sister, that was probably the right decision."

"Still, Apollo," she said, "if he's going to go out on a risky job . . . maybe I should've spent the dinner period with the guy."

"Hey, he's not going to be gone that long." He patted her slim back. "You'll have plenty of other opportunities to fend off his advances."

"I suppose," she answered, not sounding quite convinced.

Starbuck forgot to light his cigar.

Standing at the huge view window in the large dining room of the Rising Star's restaurant, arm around the slender waist of the fair Cassiopea, he watched as the onetime interstellar liner moved free of the asteroid dust.

As hundreds of new stars became visible, glittering in the blackness, the patrons of the place exclaimed, murmured, made awed noises.

"It's exciting," said Cassiopea. "Like being born into a whole new world. Aren't you excited?"

He gave his straw-colored hair a scratch. "Well, I'll tell you, Cass," he said, his unlit cigar tilting higher. "Stars and new galaxies and such do thrill me. But for real, unadulterated excitement I prefer the company of lovely ladies. Such as you."

The young woman's nose wrinkled slightly. "You aren't very poetic."

"Sure I am," he said. "Want to hear me recite some limericks? There was a—"

"Spare me," she requested, returning her gaze to the new galaxy that the *Galactica* and the ships of the fleet were entering.

Other couples who'd come to the window drifted back to their tables. Starbuck caught the eye of a pink-faced, white-haired waiter standing nearby.

The waiter eased closer and bowed. "One is reminded of the old days aboard the Rising Star," he confided with a sigh. "Before the war."

"Before the war?"

"Back before it interfered with our annual run to Quatora," explained the waiter. "Ah, there was a magnificent cluster. Seven red stars, one blue. Quite a crowd pleaser—fair took one's breath away. Filled one with a blooming sense of awe, if you know what I mean, sir."

"*You* obviously," said Cassiopea, "have a poetic soul."

The waiter smiled. "One surely likes to think so, miss. After all, to journey through life without a—"

"What we'd like even more than a poetic soul," cut in Lieutenant Starbuck as he lit his cigar, "is a private dining room."

Touching his chest, the plump waiter sighed again. "One fears that—"

"You see," said Starbuck, letting his cigar droop, "I've . . . well, I don't really like to talk about it, but . . . I've got a big mission coming up. Might be a heck of a long time before I get back here for dinner."

"Ah, one sympathizes, Lieutenant," said the waiter. "Yet, you see, private rooms are reserved six and seven millicentons in advance and so . . . hm."

Starbuck deftly transferred a gold coin from his hand to that of the waiter. "You'd be doing a good deed," he said.

"Yes, one can always make an exception for a warrior on his last night." He started to move off. "Right this way, please."

"Last night?" Starbuck's left eye narrowed. "I don't quite like the way he said that."

CHAPTER TWO

The private dining room was small, its walls and ceiling colored a pale blue. The single oval window showed the star field through which they were traveling.

Cassiopea asked, "What's all this about a mission?"

After flicking ashes from the tip of his cigar and grinning across the table at her, Starbuck replied, "Just a routine recon jaunt actually. But I figured if I dramatized it some, we'd get this more intimate—"

"Don't put on an act for me," the young woman told him. "I have a feeling you really are about to embark on a danger—"

"Nope. What's dangerous for your average warrior, Cass my love, ain't necessarily so for a member of the Starbuck clan." He took a puff of his stogie. "Let's forget all the perils and hazards that may lie in my path and—"

"Your bottle of Ambrosa, Lieutenant," said the waiter as he eased unobtrusively into their little room. "One was fortunate to find this in the Rising Star wine cellar, since Ambrosa is as rare as Tilinium or the proverbial—"

"I appreciate it, too." Starbuck passed him another coin.

"One is most grateful." He walked backwards toward the doorway. "Buzz when you are ready to order your meal."

Cassiopea watched Starbuck opening the Ambrosa container. "What exactly is your mission?"

"Told you, Cass, a simple recon run."

She pushed back from the table. "I'd like to freshen up a bit," she said, smiling. "Then I'll be right back."

Starbuck said, "Every moment apart from you is an eternity."

"Well, I shouldn't be gone more than four or five eternities."

The door opened and closed and Starbuck was alone.

But not for long.

The door panel whispered open again.

"Oops!" Starbuck set down the Ambrosa on the white tabletop.

Athena stepped across the threshold. "I . . . um . . . was looking for you."

Starbuck's chuckle sounded very boyish to his ears. "Wellsir, that's . . . um . . . nice," he said, watching the door panel slide shut behind her.

"I thought I'd better tell you that you may go on Red Alert," the dark-haired young woman said while taking a few tentative steps toward the table.

"Red Alert?" He put down his cigar.

"You see, Starbuck, I just learned that you'd volunteered for the recon probe," she said, eyes misting slightly. "I mean, you'd asked me to spend your last night with you and—"

"Why does everybody keep saying that?"

"Beg pardon?"

"Never mind."

"Guess I'm not putting this just right, Starbuck," continued Athena. "The thing is, I really don't want you to be alone. You are alone, aren't you?"

He popped to his feet, causing the table to rattle, the Ambrosa to gurgle, the two wine glasses to tinkle and the trail of smoke climbing thinly up from his stogie to zigzag. "Alone? Well . . . yes, of course."

"There are two glasses on the—"

"Talk about extrasensory perception," he chuckled, gesturing at the little room. "I was sitting here brooding, contemplating the vast panorama of this new galaxy and reflecting on the meaning of life when I got this very strong hunch that someone, someone lovely, was going to join me." He came scooting around the table to grab hold of her elbow. "That's when I ordered a second glass."

"How much of that Ambrosa have you already had?"

"Hm? None, not a drop, Athena my love," Starbuck assured her, trying to urge her doorward. "It's just you that intoxicate me. Now, if you'll just trot along with me."

"Where?"

"Where?" Starbuck blinked. "Oh, yes, to a private dining room where we can be—"

"This *is* a private dining room."

"Aw, but this one is drafty and the view is definitely second—"

"You don't get drafts in a controlled aircirc system. Are you sure you—"

"Holy mulrooney!" he suddenly exclaimed as the door hissed open. "Listen, I can explain . . . ah, hello."

"It occurred to one," said the entering waiter, "that the stalwart lieutenant might be in need of one."

"He is," confirmed Starbuck. "This dinky little private room was sufficient when I was alone and sulking. Now, though, I feel the need of something a mite better. Posher, more conducive to—"

"Ah, that may be most difficult, sir. One isn't at all certain that—"

"I'm sure you can come up with something." Starbuck passed him a coin.

"It occurs to one, Lieutenant, that there is indeed another room available, one that more ideally suits your present needs." He tapped his temple with the hand that clutched Starbuck's latest contribution. "Yet one's poor old brain is having trouble recalling—"

"This may jog it." Starbuck provided yet another glittering coin.

"It all comes back to one now, yes," said the waiter with a positive nod of his head. "Right this way, sir and miss." He bowed and led them from the room.

"You certainly seem jittery tonight," observed Athena as she took his arm. "Worrying about the mission, are you, Starbuck?"

"No, no," he said quickly. "No, it's actually the sight of you. Yes, you, the fairest creature on all the ships in the fleet. You set my blood to racing and—"

"Well, that's very flattering," she said, smiling. "Even though I don't believe it at . . . careful!"

He'd been glancing from left to right, alert, on the lookout for Cassiopea, and had tripped on a wrinkle in the carpeting. "Sorry," he said. "Being with you, love, makes me a mite giddy, I guess."

"Ah, romance," sighed the waiter.

The communication screen in Commander Adama's quarters buzzed. Leaving the comfortable chair he'd been sitting in, he moved over to it and activated the respond toggle. "Yes?"

Colonel Tigh's face appeared on the screen. "Looks like we've got something," he said. "Long-range probe indicates possible life forms in Quadrant Alpha Six."

Nodding, Adama asked, "Cylons?"

"Can't tell if it's Cylons or a friendly life form," answered Tigh. "That'll take a Recon Viper."

"Very well, get Recon Viper One ready."

"Concentrated probe indicates definite life signs," amplified the colonel. "Asteroid concentration, binary star system Alpha Six, mark 775."

"That's within a hectare of our course," said the commander.

"It is, and there's no way of knowing just what kind of life is waiting there."

"We'll find out." Breaking the connection, Commander Adama glanced toward his window. "I hope the lieutenant's finished his dinner."

After glancing around the pale green private dining room, Athena turned her attention to Starbuck. "How's this one suit you?"

"Eh?"

"Posher, less drafty?"

"Oh, sure, yes. Much better. Cosier, too." He grinned. "Of course, when I'm with you I lose all touch with my surroundings anyway."

"So I notice."

"This certainly has turned into an interesting . . . by gosh!" He'd straightened up in his padded chair and snapped his fingers. "I left the Ambrosa and my cigar in that other room." He shot up. "I'll go fetch—"

"You can ask the waiter to—"

"Nope, he strikes me as the sort of fellow who'd take a nip." Starbuck headed for the door. "Or a puff."

"Nobody in his right mind would try to smoke one of those foul cigars of yours."

"Even so." Letting himself out, he went loping back to the other private dining room.

Cassiopea was once again seated at the table, somewhat perplexed. "Where've you been? I was worried for a moment that you'd been alerted to—"

"It was too warm in here," he explained, dropping into the chair across the table from her. "I went to tell our waiter that—"

"If anything, it seems a bit chilly."

"Listen, love, let's not quibble at a time like this." Smiling, he picked up the Ambrosa and poured some into the two glasses. "Let's drink a toast to our relationship."

Their glasses clinked.

After sipping, Cassiopea said, "Very nice."

Starbuck was scowling. "No, nope. This stuff tastes less than a year old. Has a flavor like the fluid they clean spaceboots with."

"Tastes perfectly—"

"I'll go find the waiter and complain." Starbuck was on his feet again, Ambrosa bottle in hand.

"You can simply buzz the man."

"Be more efficient if I track him down, then go to their alleged wine cellar with him."

Starbuck was halfway to the door when a voxbox in the ceiling mentioned his name.

"Lieutenant Starbuck. Attention, Lieutenant Starbuck. Return to *Battlestar Galactica* at once. Lieutenant Starbuck, report to flight deck blue. Priority red!"

"Oh, Starbuck," said Cassiopea sadly. "That really glitches up our evening."

"Duty calls, love." Returning to the table, he bent and kissed her. "Stay right here for a moment, Cass. I want to carry that image away with me."

"But I—"

"Don't move. Farewell."

Outside he trotted back to the other dining room.

"Starbuck," said Athena as he came bounding in. "Did you hear the—"

"Yes, my love," he replied. "I'm afraid duty calls." Hurrying over to her, he kissed her.

"I'm going to miss you," she said.

"Same here. These moments with you have been the high point of the evening," he assured Athena. "Well, I can't linger."

She started to rise. "I'll see you to—"

"No, don't move a muscle. I want to remember you just as you are. Framed here in our little bower, a myriad of new stars behind you."

He spun on his heel and dashed out of the room.

Starbuck nearly collided with the waiter. "Oops, excuse it."

"Quite all right, sir. And might one add that one admires the lieutenant's daring?"

"Actually, this sort of mission isn't all that—"

"Not the mission, sir. The deft and audacious way you juggled the two young ladies. Ah, it took me back to the halcyon days when this liner plied the . . . alas!"

"What?"

"Both ladies are exiting from their respective cubicles. Might one suggest a hasty retreat?"

"One might indeed." Looking only at the nearest exit, Starbuck took his leave.

CHAPTER THREE

The new Recon Viper sat on a launching deck, being
readied for takeoff by a hangar crew. Watching were
Apollo and Lieutenant Boomer.

"I understand," said the black lieutenant, "that our
boy Starbuck had himself quite a farewell dinner over
on the Rising Star."

"He knows how to go in style."

An elevator door wooshed open and Starbuck, clad
in moderately flamboyant civilian garb, emerged.
"Greetings, gents," he said as he came trotting over
to them, cigar between his teeth.

"Wow, you sure do look fetching," observed
Boomer.

Starbuck held out his arms at his sides and executed
a slow turn. "What the well-dressed civilian will wear,"
he said. "Commander's idea. In case I have to land,
we don't want anyone to know who I am."

"I could spot you as Starbuck," said Boomer, "once I got a whiff of that weed you're puffing."

"Despite my fame in the fleet, folks in this galaxy don't know my trademark." He puffed on the stogie, exhaled smoke. "The important thing is that nobody tumbles that I'm a warrior."

Captain Apollo said, "You dined with Athena, huh? Among others."

Shaking his head, the lieutenant replied, "You lads don't have this problem, but there *are* those of us who are just too charming. We attract women the way a magnet attracts iron." He shrugged. "I'm looking forward to a few centons in space. Alone. Just me, a fast ship and a fair galaxy."

Nodding at Recon Viper One, Apollo said, "Well, you've got the fast ship, old buddy. Our engineers have doubled her range and speed."

Starbuck gave the new ship an admiring look as Apollo continued. "You've also got a voice-activated computer that can outfly anything the Cylons can throw at you."

After puffing on his cigar, the lieutenant said, "Do I look like I need electronic help to outfly those lunk-heads?"

"You look," said Boomer, "like you need all the help you can get."

The crew had moved away from the reconnaissance ship. The crew chief nodded once, briskly, to Apollo.

"Ready to go," Apollo told Starbuck.

"You sure? I mean, doesn't anybody have one more nasty dig to make about my social life or my flying prowess?"

"Aw, don't be glum." Boomer patted him on the

back. "You ought to know our kidding masks a deep respect for you."

"Hooey." Starbuck strode over to the waiting ship and climbed into the cockpit.

Apollo went over and watched him strapping in. "Switch on your short-range marker beacon after launch so we can track you," he said. "Other than that you shouldn't make any transmissions unless absolutely necessary, and then only in short pulse, scrambled code. We don't want the Cylons to—"

"Gee, Uncle Apollo, thanks for telling me all this," cut in Starbuck. "Me, a green kid who's never been up in a—"

"Sorry. I know you know how to handle yourself, old buddy," said the captain. "I'm concerned about you."

"Cut it out or you'll bring tears to my eyes."

"You'll love the ship," said Apollo. "They put a second pulse generator on all the engines."

"She doesn't look any bigger."

"She isn't."

Starbuck glanced around. "Yeah, but you can't add that much weight without getting rid of something."

"They removed the laser generators." Apollo helped shut him inside the cabin and then stepped away. "Ready to launch."

Starbuck automatically ran through the launching procedures. "Sure, that makes sense," he said to himself. "You remove the laser generators and you cut down on the weight."

As the Viper went roaring through the launch tube and into space Starbuck realized what that meant.

"Hey, this jalopy is unarmed!"

• • •

Lieutenant Boomer turned away from the viewport in the launch area. "Sort of wish we were tagging along with him."

"Yep, so do I," said Apollo. "This could be a risky trip for Starbuck."

"Hope he doesn't run into any big trouble."

"Well, even though the new Viper is unarmed, it has other advantages," the captain assured him. "It's faster than anything he's likely to encounter."

"Trouble is, we can't be sure just exactly what Starbuck is going to run into," reminded Boomer. "This galaxy's new to us."

"Well, Starbuck can handle just about any situation."

Boomer grinned. "One thing I'll bet on," he said. "If there're any women out there, Starbuck'll find 'em."

"Matter of fact," said Apollo, "he's sort of got a woman along with him."

Boomer frowned. "How's that again?"

"Didn't I tell you about Cora?" asked Apollo.

CHAPTER FOUR

Starbuck was impressed.

He'd been taking the new Viper through a series of rolls, loops and banks. The trim little ship was performing better than any craft he'd ever handled.

Settling back, the lieutenant lit a fresh cigar.

"Ahem."

He sat up. "Who the heck is that?"

"If you're finished with your stunting, dear heart, how about we get cracking on our mission?" A throaty feminine voice issued from a voxgrid on the control dash.

Starbuck removed his cigar from between his teeth. "Do I know you?"

"I'm your computer, hon."

"Hey, I didn't turn you on. A computer isn't supposed to just come popping on when—"

"Oh, don't be a fuddy duddy."

"A what?"

"You wouldn't think much of a computer who doesn't speak up when she wants to, would you? Heck, no. After all, sweets, the whole notion of my being just a sort of servant is really—"

"Whoa now," he cut in. "Suppose you try addressing me as Lieutenant Starbuck? Or sir. There's a certain protocol to this sort of—"

"Nertz," replied the computer. "Who are you trying to impress, Starbuck? I've read through your record and, seems to me, protocol and dignity are things that you steer clear of. There was that time, for instance, when they found you in the Nurses' Dorm with—"

"You have access to my personnel records? Is that standard operating—"

"Who said anything about my being standard equipment? Honestly. Now, let me introduce myself. You can call me Cora."

"Cora?"

"CORA. It stands for Computer/Oral Response Activated," explained Cora. "Now that the ice's been broken, shall we concentrate on our mission?"

"I got a couple of oral responses I'd like to try on you, sister."

"Beg pardon?"

Starbuck stuck his cigar back in his mouth. "I've been trying to concentrate on the mission," he informed the computer. "But you, you keep babbling like a teenager at a pajama party or—"

"I like the way your voice sounds when you get angry."

"I'm not angry! I never get angry! I am known far and wide for the exceptional calm I exhibit even under the most trying circumstances!"

After a snickering laugh, the computer fell silent for a moment. Then Cora said, "We are on a Delta vector for Quadrant Alpha Six. I've activated my sensors and I'm probing the asteroid area where life forms were reported by the *Galactica*'s rather limited scanners."

"Vanity, vanity."

"Seems silly to be falsely modest about your gifts," said the computer. "I'm picking up two unidentified sublight vehicles. Bearing is Omega One, Alpha Six. Shall we poke our nose into it farther, Starbuck?"

"Well, that's what we're here for, Cora," he said, exhaling smoke. "But if these unidentified objects turn out to be Cylons, I'm going to feel downright silly about not having any weapons."

"Oh, we have enough speed to outrun anything in the universe."

"So you say."

Cora snorted. "Nothing to worry about, love. Just hang on and I'll take us over for a looksee."

"Well, hon?" asked Cora.

They had slowed to sublight speed.

Starbuck was watching a viscreen on the dash panel. Absently he flicked ashes from his cigar. "Both of them are ancient, real antiques."

"You really, if you don't mind my saying so, ought to try to maintain a neater cockpit. This is a brand new ship and already you've scattered—"

"Hush," he advised. "Let's concentrate on the matter at hand."

On the screen he saw a venerable, battered shuttlecraft. Its markings were faded and it was executing some shaky evasive actions to keep clear of the equally ancient starfighter that was trailing it and firing intermittent bursts. Neither ship was as yet aware that the Recon Viper was approaching.

"I'd estimate," said the computer, "that both the shuttle and the pursuit ship date back to the sixth millenium at least. I couldn't begin to guess the origins of either."

"It isn't likely, though, that they're Cylons."

"Unless the Cylons have had some budget cuts we don't know about, no."

"That shuttle's unarmed, and I don't much like the idea of an unarmed craft being chased by a fighter." Starbuck took a quick puff of his stogie. "And it's going to futz up my report on the life forms hereabouts if somebody kills some of 'em."

"I have a plan, Bucky. Suppose we—"

"Don't," Starbuck warned, "ever call me Bucky."

"What then? Starsy?"

"Lieutenant Starbuck, sir. Try that."

"Two people traveling in a small intimate vehicle shouldn't be so darn formal."

"Quit gabbing and get to the point, Cora."

"I was about to suggest a high speed flyby, Lieutenant Starbuck, sir," said the computer. "We'll kick in our second booster within fifty metrons and force the fighter off course. Should also scare the bejabbers out of him. Shall I execute?"

"Tell you what," said Starbuck, gripping the controls. "I'll fly this crate from now on. Release controls."

"But it's considerably more efficient if I—"

"Release 'em, kiddo."

Cora sighed. "Released."

CHAPTER FIVE

The pilot of the rattletrap fighter sat hunched in his seat. He was a dark, lanky man of thirty, dressed in trousers and a tunic, both of a rusty brown color. His long black hair was tied back with a twist of a crimson cord. On one breast of his tunic was a star emblem.

There was an oily, smoky smell in the battered cockpit. The image of the pursued shuttle showed fuzzy on the dirt-smeared screen of the dash scanner.

"You're not going to get away this time, Robber," the fighter pilot promised the blurred image of his prey.

He reached again toward the triggering mechanism of his guns.

"This'll fix . . . what the hell?"

Something, a fighter ship maybe, had come whizzing across his stern. The ship, like nothing he'd ever seen, had sent a dazzling blast of white sizzling from its engines.

Dazzled, confused, the pilot tried a wobbling maneuver that was intended to get him away from there.

By the time he got his fighter under control there was no sign of the shuttle he'd been chasing. And no trace of the new craft that had come flashing out of nowhere at him.

With a hand that was shaking slightly he activated his talkmike. "This is Croad," he said, anger and perplexity mixing in his voice. "Lost contact and returning to Proteus." After a moment he added, "It could just be we got us some trouble."

Starbuck grinned and relit his cigar.

The computer made a disapproving, throat-clearing sound. "Were you aware, dear heart, that you were fifty-two metrons away when you kicked in the booster?"

"So? It worked admirably, did it not, Cora my love?"

"But it was sloppy. If you'd allowed me to take care of it, which, after all, is my—"

"Let's establish once and for all who's the boss of this contraption, sis, so we—"

"Shall we get back to business? Ahem. The fighter has disengaged and is turning toward an asteroid point-seven-one mectares distant," said Cora in an efficient, schoolmarm tone.

"What about the shuttle?"

"Shuttlecraft has been damaged," replied the computer, "and has landed on an asteroid directly ahead."

Starbuck blew a thoughtful plume of smoke ceilingward. "Let us follow the shuttle," he said. "I'm curious as to why that fighter was so darn anxious to destroy it."

"May I land us?" inquired Cora. "Or do we have to have a landing rife with rattles, bounces, jiggles and—"

"Do you know what feathers are?"

"Certainly, hon. I know just about everything there is to know, since I—"

"When I set this crate down on yonder asteroid, you'll think we're settling into a bed of soft, downy feathers."

"That I'll believe when—"

"Just give me the damn vectors for a landing."

"Vectors displayed."

Teeth chomping on his cigar, Starbuck concentrated on setting the Viper down.

Starbuck unhooked his safety gear and looked out through the cockpit window. "How'd you like the landing, Cora?"

"Passable," answered the computer.

The asteroid was bleak, a blend of dark, pocked rock and grey scruffy brush. There was a gaping cavemouth nearby and a few indications that, years ago, this asteroid had been mined. The downed shuttle was just beyond the next rise.

"Atmosphere outside acceptable," said Cora. "You won't need any special gear."

He nodded. "How many folks aboard the shuttle?"

"One. Humanoid life form. No laser weapons."

Patting his holster, the lieutenant said, "Guess I'll mosey over and introduce myself. Seems the neighborly thing to do."

"Be careful."

"Your concern is touching."

"I don't need you to fly off this hunk of rock, hon,"

said the computer. "But if I show up back at the *Galactica* with your lifeless carcass, it'll be a black mark on—"

"Fear not, Cora. I fully intend to return in the same pristine condition I am now." He opened the hatch.

"Switching all systems, except marker beacon, to standby mode." Starbuck stepped free of the Viper. As his booted feet touched the rocky ground, the door whispered shut behind him.

He hunched his shoulders once. It was chilly. The sky was a star-filled black. The abandoned drillbot by the cave opening lay on its side, brush tangled around its battered exterior.

Starbuck was still several yards from the downed shuttle, lasergun in hand, when he heard a metallic bonging. He approached cautiously.

The ship really was a relic, its hull pitted and dented. Two booted feet stuck out from beneath the shuttle. The banging came from there. An open tool chest sat near the protruding feet.

"You just drop in to gawk?" asked the owner of the feet. "Or are you maybe going to pitch in and help?"

Starbuck took a step back. "Help," he managed to answer.

"Then hand me that damn deltoid spanner there, will you?" From beneath the ship slid a tall, slender young woman of twenty-two or so. Her trousers were splotched with white paint. A patch of tanned skin showed through a hole in her tunic, and her jacket looked as though it had barely escaped a fire. She was pretty, though, with long dark hair. "Are you through ogling me?"

Starbuck considered her question. "For now," he answered and passed her the tool she'd requested.

The young woman wiped the heel of her hand across her perspiring forehead, leaving behind a fresh gritty streak. "That ought to do it. The damage done by my quick landing's all fixed up," she said, giving the shuttle a kick and then tossing the electrowrench she'd been using to Starbuck. "Pack that, will you?"

"Who was that on your tail?" He deposited the wrench in the tool locker.

She shrugged. "Pirate. Probably from the Hohne System," she replied. "They're all nasty, mercenary bastards thereabouts. I should've known better than to shortcut across this particular asteroid belt." She held out a grease-stained right hand. "By the way, my name's Robber."

"Robber? That's not the most feminine name I've—"

"What's yours?"

"Starbuck."

Robber gave a left-shouldered shrug, then brushed her dark hair back. "Your name's not all that nifty either," she observed. "Anyway, thanks for scaring that pirate bastard off." She yanked the door of her shuttle open and reached inside.

Automatically Starbuck's hand swung to his holster.

"Relax, Starbuck," the young woman said, laughing. "I've got no designs on your person. Care for a drink?"

"Well, I suppose after our shared ordeal . . . what the heck's that?"

She'd produced a flask of amber liquor from her cabin. Unstopping it, she took a swig. "Ambrosa," she answered as she wiped the flaskmouth with the tattered sleeve of her jacket. "Don't they have it where you hail from?"

"We do, sure, but it's sort of expensive and..." He accepted the bottle and drank. "Hey, this stuff is aged. Where did you get hold of—"

"Oh, just a little bonus my boss gave me," Robber told him. "And now, Starbuck, I'd better finish hauling this load of agritools to the farmers on Croton. Otherwise, no more bonuses."

Starbuck took a further sip. "This stuff is amazing," he said.

"Keep the bottle."

"Well, thanks."

"After all, you sort of saved me from being highjacked," she said. "Or worse. Some of these pirates are in cahoots with slavers." She flipped him the flask stopper.

"I'm curious about—"

"You know, Starbuck, I think I have time to take a quick look at your ship," the young woman said. "I only got a glimpse, but it seemed like nothing I've ever run into."

"It's different, all right, but..."

Robber laughed again. "Don't trust me?"

Starbuck said, "Okay, c'mon. I'll give you the short tour."

He noticed, as she walked beside him toward his Viper, that she was as tall as he was.

When they passed the abandoned mine, Starbuck asked, "Does this particular asteroid have a name or—"

"Got me, Starbuck. I'm merely passing through."

"But you knew where to land."

"Hell, you have to with an old clunker like mine," she explained. "I've got emergency landing spots charted all over my run," Robber said. "But I can't fill you in on the local history of a damned one."

They reached the Viper and Starbuck opened the door. "Welcome to my humble home." He gestured at the interior with his hand.

She moved up beside him, glancing inside. "Damn, that's really something," she said admiringly. "Latest stuff, all in perfect shape."

"Before you rush back to your shuttle," he said, "I'd like to ask you a few questions about—"

"I don't have much time for small talk," she said. "Tell you what, though, walk me over to my crate and I'll dig out another bottle of Ambrosa for you."

"Another one?"

"You might as well have it, as a souvenir of our chance meeting."

"That's mighty thoughtful of you." He turned, ready for the return trip.

That's when she hit him behind the ear with something cold and metallic.

CHAPTER SIX

The dark-haired young woman stepped back from Starbuck's sprawled, unconscious body. Hands on hips, she said, "Sorry, since you don't seem like a bad guy. But Croad is most likely still hunting for me out there and I need something a hell of a lot faster than my old shuttle."

Bending, she grabbed him under the arms and dragged him across the rocky ground until he was a safe distance from the Viper. She turned and walked over to the ship.

Robber climbed into the cockpit. After brushing cigar ash off the seat, she settled in at the controls.

Before shutting the door, she took a farewell look out at Starbuck. "You'll be okay here till we come back for my cargo," she said. "Right now I have to concentrate on ditching Croad."

Hunching in the seat, she studied the controls. Brow

furrowed, she drummed her grease-stained fingers on the dash. "Sure, I can handle this thing," Robber decided after a moment or two. "Got a voice-activated computer, too. Hey, wake up!"

Cora said, "Are we ready to go, Starbuck?"

"Can you fly this crate?"

"Who the dickens are you?"

"Never mind. Just—"

"Where's Starbuck? What've you done with him, you floozie?"

Robber made an exasperated noise. "Forget it. I'll do the flying myself."

"I should've known. I let him out of my sight and he takes up with some featherbrained—"

"Off. Turn yourself off."

"First, sister, you tell me exactly what—"

"Off."

The computer, since she was programmed to obey verbal orders, turned off.

Robber rubbed her hands together. "Now, let's see if I can really handle a first class ship."

Commander Adama moved through the bridge of the *Galactica* until he stood beside Athena. "What's the latest word on Lieutenant Starbuck?"

"The short-range marker indicates Recon Viper One is climbing back into orbit."

"Very well," the commander said to his daughter. "Maintain tracking. He may be on to something."

"Probably a blonde."

"What's that?"

"Thinking out loud, sorry. I didn't mean . . . wait. Something new is happening."

Resting a hand on her shoulder, he leaned closer

to the screen. Frowning at the information that was being displayed there, he said, "I don't quite understand this."

"Long-range transmissions are being sent from Starbuck's Viper."

"Long-range?"

"Narrow-beam," she replied. "It...seems to be some sort of code. But not scrambled."

Colonel Tigh came over. "What the devil is Starbuck up to?"

"Perhaps," suggested Adama, "his short-pulse transmitter is inoperative."

"That's possible," said Athena, stroking her cheek as she watched the console screen. "But why would he use an unknown code? And why send the message unscrambled?"

"I suggest," said Tigh, "that we check the Cylon codes."

Nodding, Adama said, "We have to check every possibility."

Athena punched instructions into her machine. A moment passed and then her answer appeared. "Whatever the code is, it's not in any known Cylon pattern," she said. "Which means Starbuck's ship hasn't been grabbed by any enemy—"

"We still have to assume," said the black colonel, "that someone has taken over Starbuck's Viper. Cylon or Cylon sympathizer, we don't know at this point. The important thing to keep in mind is that Starbuck isn't in control."

"It could be Starbuck," said Athena, "who's sending this message, Colonel. True, we don't know why he's using this particular code, but maybe—"

"If that isn't a message to the Cylons, Athena,"

said Tigh, "it's at least a beacon that can lead them to this galaxy."

"I just think it's too soon to jump to the concl—"

"We have to stop that transmission," said Colonel Tigh quietly.

Athena said nothing, glancing up at her father.

Commander Adama said, "Alert Apollo."

Lieutenant Boomer came hurrying along a launching area walkway to Captain Apollo. "What the hell is going on?"

"We've got us a somewhat tricky assignment," answered Apollo.

"Yeah, that I know." The black lieutenant glanced at the two Viper ships that were being readied for takeoff. "What kind of mess is Starbuck in this time?"

"That's what we can maybe find out."

"Yeah, but they got to be kidding about our orders, huh?" said Boomer. "We're supposed to be prepared to destroy Recon Viper One. What if Starbuck's still in the damn thing?"

"It looks sort of like he isn't."

"Meaning what?"

Apollo started walking toward the nearly ready ships. "I wish I knew," he said. "But it could be . . . could be he's dead. That somebody took over his—"

"C'mon. Starbuck's not that easy to kill." Boomer walked alongside the captain. "What we got to do is try to establish communications with the ship when we find it—see what's going on."

"The best we can do, good buddy, is give him a chance to identify himself," said Apollo. "If he doesn't, then the assumption has to be that the Viper's been taken over. We have to destroy it."

"Somebody could have taken it over and still maybe have him in there. We destroy—"

"I don't like this any better than you," said Apollo, stopping next to his craft. "If Starbuck's not in the ship and if we destroy it, we may never learn where he is. Unfortunately, being warriors, we have to follow orders."

"Listen, that Viper isn't even armed. So if somebody's using it, they can't really—"

"It wasn't armed when it left the *Galactica*, Boomer. We don't really have any idea what state it's in now."

"Seems unlikely anybody could've—"

"We don't want the ship falling into enemy hands," said Apollo. "And if somebody's taken it away from Starbuck, we have to assume they're enemies."

Boomer walked over to his ship. "Hell," he remarked.

CHAPTER SEVEN

Starbuck made a noise.

It was a rude noise, suggesting disappointment with his current position in life. He had just awakened to find himself sprawled, face down, on the uncomfortable surface of a small-time asteroid in the middle of nowhere. And the back of his head hurt.

"Darn that female grease monkey," he muttered as he pushed himself to a sitting position. His stomach started doing loops inside him.

Spilled out beside him was the Ambrosa.

After making another unhappy noise, Starbuck got to his feet.

Slowly, he turned toward his Viper.

"Frack," he remarked.

The ship, Cora and all, was gone.

Starbuck looked up into the dark sky. "Out of the kindness of my heart I stop to aid a damsel in distress," he said in a moderately self-pitying tone. "I try to do a good deed and what do I get? A bop on the head." Very gingerly, he touched the spot where Robber had slugged him.

"Should've known better," he muttered, starting to pace, "than to trust a woman named Robber. I mean, now that I think about it, that's not a name to inspire confidence. But me, I open up my ship, show her its luxurious interior and then turn my stupid back on her."

He kicked at the empty Ambrosa flask.

"Behaved like a green rookie. Take a drink from a stranger, let her knock me out. Guess I'm lucky she didn't swipe my pants, too."

The best thing to do, he decided, was to stop feeling sorry for himself, and quit being mad at Robber. None of that would get him anywhere.

"She was sort of pretty, though."

It was thoughts like that that'd got him in trouble in the first place. If Robber had been a grizzled male spacehauler, he'd never have turned his back.

"Right now, hot shot," Starbuck reminded himself, "what we have to do is get off this particular chunk of real estate."

He trotted over the rise to Robber's shuttle. At least that was still there.

"Maybe I can track that lady down and retrieve my Viper," he said as he opened the door to the shuttle's cabin. "Yep, I'm going to have to do something like that. Because I sure as heck don't want to go limping back to the *Galactica* in this thing and tell 'em a girl barely out of her teens stole my buggy."

The cabin wasn't much. It smelled of oil and fuel and old age. A clay flowerpot perched on the control panel, holding what might be a geranium. A length of scarlet ribbon was tangled around the talkmike.

"Flying this clunker is going to be like taking part in a historical pageant on the early days of space flight."

Starbuck lit a fresh cigar and sat in the pilot seat.

The controls were simple, primitive in fact, and presented no problem.

The only trouble was that Starbuck couldn't get the damn shuttle to start. It occurred to him that Robber, who'd probably been planning to steal his ship all along, had only pretended that the shuttle was fixed.

"Conned again," he said, sighing out smoke.

Starbuck just about had the damage to the engines of the ancient shuttle repaired. He came sliding from underneath the crate to get a new wrench.

"I can still catch up with that . . . oops."

A lanky, weatherbeaten man in russet clothes was standing beside the shuttle. There was a silvery star emblazoned on the left breast pocket of his jacket and a laser pistol in his right hand. "You're a new one," he said.

"I am, yes. A tourist actually, simply passing through your galaxy."

"Where's Robber?"

"I wish I knew, Mr. . . . ?"

"Croad's my name. Enforcer Croad."

"I'm Starbuck," he said, attempting a friendly and cordial smile. "See, I set down here in my own ship to see what was wrong with this shuttle and . . . well, what with one thing and another I ended up somewhat stranded. So I've been putting this crate back into—"

"Where's Robber?"

Starbuck said, "As I told you, I don't know."

"Maybe when you get to Proteus you'll be in a more talkative mood."

"I sort of doubt that," said Starbuck. "The lady borrowed my ship. I haven't, really, much of an idea where she's gotten to. You're the local law, huh?"

"Are you pretending you don't know that?" Croad's laugh was cold and thin.

"Well, as I explained, I'm only passing through, Croad, and I'm not up on the—"

"Enforcer Croad."

"Enforcer Croad. The point is, I'm a stranger here myself," said the lieutenant.

"And I suppose you don't even know what Robber's tub is hauling?"

"Oh, that I know," said Starbuck, brightening. "Farm implements."

"Inside." Croad gestured at the shuttle's open cabin doorway with his gun hand.

"Sure, but—"

"Get on in there, Starbuck. Fast."

Shrugging, he complied. "Not all that cozy in here, is it? Myself I prefer—"

"Open, very slowly and carefully, that door to the cargo chamber."

"Okay." Starbuck crossed to the metal door and tugged it open.

Inside the hold were dozens of wooden crates, each labeled *Agritools*.

"See? Just like I said."

"Bring one of those crates outside."

Picking up a crate, Starbuck hefted it out into the open. "Funny that farm tools'd gurgle when you heft 'em," he observed, depositing the crate on the ground.

"Use that crowbar from the tool chest there," ordered Croad, pointing with is gun barrel. "Open the thing."

"You know, I've seen farm tools before," said Starbuck, hesitating, "and they're not that exciting."

"Open it. Quit stalling."

"Okay, sure." He used the metal bar to lift the lid off the wooden box. "Darn."

There were no tools inside. Instead he saw eight full bottles of Ambrosa resting on straw.

"You know what the penalty for hauling this stuff is?" asked the lawman.

"No, but I bet I'm going to find out," answered Starbuck.

CHAPTER EIGHT

Starbuck stooped and picked up the crate that didn't contain farm tools. "I suppose you'll want to take this along as evidence," he said, carrying it closer to the lawman.

"Put it down," ordered Croad. "I'm sending a crew back here to pick up the whole damn cargo."

"But don't you think we better take at least this one along in your—"

"No. Drop it, Starbuck."

"Well, okay." He appeared to stumble and when he dropped the heavy crate, he dropped it on Croad's foot.

"Damn it to—"

Dodging to one side, Starbuck then dived at him.

Croad's gun had swung wide at the moment the crate hit him. Before he could swing it back toward Starbuck the lieutenant jabbed him hard in the stomach with an elbow. Then he grabbed Croad's gun wrist.

"Hate to defy the law," said Starbuck apologetically, "but..."

Using Croad's arm as a lever, he flipped the man to the ground.

Croad's breath came wooshing out on impact.

Starbuck wrenched the lasergun from his grip, tossed it aside. Then he delivered two impressive jabs to Croad's chin.

The lanky lawman went slack, settled out on his back.

After gathering up the gun, Starbuck dragged the unconscious man over to the shuttle. "Think I saw some rope in the cabin that'll do for trussing you up for a spell," he said. "Then, since borrowing seems to be so popular in these parts, I'm going to take your fighter and go find the dear young lady who started this whole darn mess."

"What a clunker," remarked Starbuck as he set a landing pattern for the borrowed fighter.

He'd been able to use the old-fashioned tracking gear in the lawman's ship to get a fix on his missing Viper. The craft had landed on a lush green planetoid.

"I really want to meet that larcenous lady again," he said, lighting a fresh cigar. "Conks me on the dome, leaves me on a dinky asteroid with her disabled shuttle. *And* leaves me holding a cargo of hot Ambrosa."

He wondered where the stuff came from. Aged Ambrosa of that quality wasn't easy to come by and here was this duplicitous girl rattling around with a whole ship full of the stuff.

"Imagine what that'd be worth on the open market."

Starbuck had a brief image of himself as a bootlegger. With that shuttle full of Ambrosa he could set up in business and . . .

"Nope, my unfortunate handicap prevents me," he reminded himself. "I'm basically honest, darn it."

He was coming in above fields of grain and high, nearly orange grass that fluttered gently in a mild breeze. And there, in a clearing between the fields and a sprawling forest, sat his Viper.

Starbuck took a satisfied puff on his cigar. "Got you now, Robber."

Starbuck set the borrowed fighter down a hundred yards from his recon ship. He stayed in the cabin for a moment, eyes narrowed and scanning the area.

A faint breeze rustled the high grass on his left. To his right a forest of tangle-branched trees rose high and silent. Overhead three pale green birds circled and drifted.

"Well, let's have our showdown and get it over with." He climbed free of the fighter, gun drawn, and stood facing the Viper.

The cockpit door hung open. There was no sign of anyone inside.

Cautiously Starbuck approached the ship. The green birds high above cawed and shrieked. The whole area felt empty, deserted.

"Where the heck is she?"

He stalked up to the cockpit, breath held, and looked inside.

Empty.

"Cora," he said to the computer, "what's up?"

The computer responded, "Is that you, Starbuck?"

"Who else?"

"Well, it's a load off my mind. I really thought that dreadful hussy had—"

"Where is she?"

"Are you okay, hon? I've been worried silly, because I didn't know if she'd done you in or simply abandoned you. I've been sitting here trying to figure out how to repair the Viper so I could go back and—"

"Repair it?"

"Now don't lose your temper, hon. There was a little, very minor, damage when I forced the ship to come down here instead—"

"You forced it?" He climbed into the cockpit.

"I have to tell you," the voice-activated computer told him. "It was a real conflict. Even though I'm a computer I have to abide by the basic rules of robotics. Therefore I was torn between serving her and—"

"You mean you sabotaged things after she highjacked this crate?"

"I felt awful about it, since I'm not supposed to do things like that. However, she wasn't you and so—"

"Where was she trying to get to?"

"To this planetoid, but about a hundred miles to the south. I threw a spanner into that little plan. My idea was to make the wench think the ship was on the fritz, get her outside of it and then—"

"Where is she now, what'd you do to her?"

"Is that concern I sense? How can you have any feeling for a nasty—"

"Just tell me where she is."

"Heading for home, afoot," answered Cora. "It's her intention, or so I gathered when she was ranting at me and the ship, to get some of her cronies to come back and repair the Viper. But don't bank on that. I doubt she'll make it home."

Starbuck blew out smoke. "Why not?"

"This is apparently hostile country for her. So it's nearly certain she'll be killed by some rival faction or other. . . .Sorry, I don't have all the details, but it's really not that important. One little group preys on another. It's the way of the world," said Cora. "Well, now that she's out of the way, shall we fix the Viper and get on about our—"

"You let that kid walk off into the wilds alone?"

"Starbuck, she's your enemy, remember?"

He scowled. "She is, in a way," he admitted. "But, hell, Cora, I can't let Robber get killed. She's an outlaw, sure, but—"

"Robber? Don't tell me you've gone gaga over a bimbo named Robber?"

"That's only a nickname. And underneath that tough, grease-stained exterior, she's just a young woman who—"

"A young woman who left you for dead and stole your ship, hon."

"Aw, she didn't bop me that hard. And in her place I might—"

"I can't believe my ears."

"You don't have ears."

"Metaphorically speaking. As a warrior you should have arrived here with nothing but revenge and retribution in mind."

"As a matter of fact, Cora, that is basically what I was thinking about," he said. "But. . . well, I just don't like the idea of her being out there in the wilds alone."

"You can't be foolish enough to think you can go after her and—"

"In a way, it's our fault she's in danger and so—"

"All right, suppose you do follow her? Whatever it is that's lurking in that wild wood to kill her will just end up fixing you as well."

"Nope, I can handle my—"

"How'd you get here, by the way?"

"Borrowed a lawman's fighter. That other ship we saw."

"A lawman? You mean you've already clashed with an official of the area and—"

"How long ago did she take off?"

"Not long, moments. She headed south. You'll notice her trail without—"

"Okay, wait here, Cora. This won't take long."

"Starbuck," she said as he headed for the doorway. "There's something else you ought to know."

"More jolly news?"

"She made a long-range call."

"To where? To who?"

"To whom is the correct—"

"Tell me."

"She was trying to contact the planet Aeries."

"But that's controlled by the Cylons. She can't be an agent for those—"

"I personally don't think she, whatever else awful she is, is a Cylon agent, no. I have the impression she doesn't even know they've overrun the planet," said Cora. "The code she used, although I haven't yet been able to break it, isn't one of the Cylons'."

Scratching his blond hair, Starbuck observed, "This is getting goofier and goofier."

"Let's forget it and get ourselves off this planetoid right now," suggested the computer. "The Cylons may have used that signal to lead some of their fighters right to us."

"That's possible, but I have to find that girl." He dropped from the ship. "See you soon."

"You're being very foolish," called Cora.

He moved away from the Viper.

CHAPTER NINE

The forest closed in on Starbuck. The thick twisted branches of the tall trees interlaced high overhead, cutting off much of the light. The brush, in dozens of shades of green and orange, grew thick and tangled on each side of the narrow trail he was following. Far off, almost lost in the dark, straight lines of trees, were faint animal rustlings and the thin cries of strange birds.

"Not my idea of an ideal vacation spot," the lieutenant said to himself.

Maybe, as the efficient Cora had pointed out, this whole thing was foolish. Robber, after all, seemed to be a pretty capable young woman. She could probably take care of herself, even in what was supposed to be hostile country.

"I wonder how exactly it's hostile," Starbuck reflected as he trekked along the forest trail. "Wild animals, wild men . . . what?"

Starbuck continued through the shadowy silence for a while, then he saw a bulky shape looming up ahead. Easing out his lasergun, he slowed his pace.

"Jitters," he said a moment later.

It was an abandoned agritractor, slumped at the edge of the trail, rusty and taken over by gnarled, large-leaved vines.

Just beyond the ancient tractor the woods ended and acre after acre of fields stretched away. Once this was farm land, a cultivated area. But that was a long time ago and the forest had been taking back the land for quite a while. The fields were overgrown with high grass and weeds. Saplings had begun to grow here and there.

About a quarter-mile to his right stood three low, sprawling buildings. Starbuck decided to take a look at them.

Weathered and peeling lettering on the front of the smallest of the three deserted buildings spelled out *Skyfarms, Ltd./Plantation 4A.*

"Business doesn't seem to be thriving," observed Starbuck as he wandered from the office to the warehouse.

Suddenly he threw himself flat out in the grass, bringing up his gun hand.

There was someone sitting on a wooden chair near the open doorway of the domed warehouse.

After watching the figure for a moment, Starbuck realized it wasn't moving at all and didn't seem to be aware of him.

Cautiously, he got to his feet and moved closer.

It was an old workbot, in roughly humanoid shape, clad in what was left of a pair of overalls. The gun-metal surface was pitted and stained. One of the plastic eyes was cracked and dangled from its socket by a twist of multicolored wire. The arms hung limply at its sides and the robot gave the impression it hadn't moved in years.

When Starbuck halted in front of the mechanism, its head gave a creaky nod. "Howdy...howdy ...howdy..." it croaked in a rusty voice and then ceased to speak or move.

"Well, howdy," said Starbuck. He walked on by and into the warehouse.

The high-ceilinged room was big and empty. A scatter of small, yellow birds was roosting on one of the rafters.

Starbuck noticed something on the dusty floor a few yards away. "Wait now," he said, trotting over to it.

He knelt and confirmed his initial impression. It was the faded jacket Robber had been wearing.

There were signs in the dust that some kind of struggle had taken place on this spot. Worse, he saw several small splashes of what had to be blood.

Apollo picked up his talkmike. "Looks like this is the place, Boomer," he said as his Viper circled low over the area on the planetoid where Starbuck's recon ship had sat down.

"That's his Viper sure enough," said Boomer from his ship. "Who do you think that rundown fighter belongs to?"

"Maybe an antique collector." They'd followed the Viper's beacon signal to the planetoid and now Apollo tried again to contact the craft. "Calling Recon Viper

One. Starbuck, are you aboard?"

"Oh, I wish he were," answered a distraught feminine voice.

"This is Captain Apollo, from the *Battlestar Galactica*," he said. "Who am I talking to?"

"Just call me Cora, Captain. I'm the computer."

"Where's Starbuck?"

"It's a long and heartrending, story."

"Is he alive?"

"He was, and I sincerely hope he still is. You see, Captain, it all began—"

"Is it safe to land?"

"Oh, yes."

"Who does that fighter belong to?"

"Well, right now to Starbuck more or less. He stole it, you see, in order to chase that dreadful outlaw girl who—"

"We'll land," Apollo informed her.

"I knew there was a woman in it someplace," commented Boomer. "Leave it to Starbuck."

"Sounds like," said Apollo, "even the darn computer has a crush on him."

Apollo sat in the cockpit of the recon ship. Boomer leaned in through the open hatch. "Calm down, Cora," the captain was telling the distraught computer.

"It's simply that I'm quite concerned about him. That's only natural, since I was built to—"

"Just fill us in," requested Apollo, "on what happened."

"He went looking for her."

"For who?"

"For whom," corrected Cora. "That awful young

woman named Robber. Can you imagine anyone going through life with—"

"Is she the one who borrowed this Viper?"

"That's what I've been trying to tell you. The hussy stole it, after poor dear Bucky had tried to help her get off that asteroid where—"

"Bucky?" Boomer laughed.

"Where's Starbuck now?" Apollo asked.

"Searching for her. I made the mistake . . . when you're programmed to be honest, it's very difficult to fib at all . . . I mentioned that she'd have to travel across hazardous country on her way home."

"What sort of hazards?"

"I'm not certain," answered Cora. "If you wish, Captain, I can run some scans of the—"

"No time for that," he cut in. "Which way did Starbuck head when he took off after this lady?"

"South, you'll see the trail yonder," the computer replied. "I told him it was foolhardy."

"That's never stopped Starbuck," said Boomer.

CHAPTER TEN

Starbuck shook the decrepit robot again by its shoulders. "What happened to the girl? What did you see?"

The weatherbeaten mechanism that sat beside the warehouse door replied, "Howdy...howdy..."

"C'mon," urged the impatient lieutenant. "You're not completely defunct. You must've seen something."

"Howdy...looks like rain, don't it?...Yep... good crop this season....Howdy, neighbor... howdy..."

Snorting, Starbuck let the robot fall back into its chair. "Thanks, you sodkicking bucket of bolts."

"...howdy...howdy..."

Starbuck stepped clear and began examining the weedy ground around the entrance of the Skyfarms warehouse. He saw bootprints from at least two pairs of feet and, unfortunately, a few more spatters of fresh blood.

"Well, I'm pretty certain I can follow this trail," Starbuck said, eyes narrowing. "I just hope to hell I find her alive at the end of it."

Slowly, carefully, he began moving away from the abandoned warehouse.

"...come see us anytime, you hear?..." rasped the robot.

The forest started closing in on Starbuck again. The smell of stagnant water was growing in the air. A thin mist came drifting at him through the trees.

Starbuck whistled for a moment, with his tongue placed against the back of his teeth.

The woodlands were getting darker, colder. The mist came twisting around his ankles in ragged ribbons.

The signs were still easy to follow. Two men had passed this way recently, one of them carrying something. Starbuck was pretty sure that something was Robber.

No way of telling whether she was alive or dead.

Shaking his head, he said to himself, "I'm really getting dippy as I grow older. Here I am getting all upset and anxious over a girl I barely know."

And it wasn't as though their brief encounter had been especially friendly or cordial. About the only thing you could say in Robber's favor was that she hadn't whacked him hard enough to crack his skull.

"She was sort of pretty, though," he reminded himself.

The mist was swirling thicker around him. Up ahead a mournful bird cried once.

Starbuck was going to have a tricky time of it when he got back to the *Galactica*. Justifying what he was doing in a report would require all his skills in the arts of propaganda and evasion.

He grinned. "Well, I wouldn't be living up to my reputation if I didn't go off on—"

"Help! Please, somebody!"

A woman's voice had called out from somewhere in the misty forest on his right.

"Don't let them hurt me!"

"Robber?" he yelled.

No reply.

Starbuck tugged his laser pistol free of its holster as he left the trail. The bluish mist tattered and broke apart as he pushed his way through it. He had a fair notion of where the cries had come from.

"Oh, please! Help me!"

Starbuck couldn't see a damn thing in the thick mist.

The voice that was calling for help sounded like Robber and yet it didn't.

"But there can't be two girls in trouble in this same patch of woods."

He had to slow down, since he could no longer see more than a few feet ahead of him.

Everything—his footfalls, the sounds of the forest—was muffled.

"Help!"

Aiming at the latest call, Starbuck quickened his pace.

After just five steps the ground opened up and swallowed him.

She was blonde and lean, not more than nineteen. She wore dark trousers, a black sleeveless tunic and a thick gunbelt that sported two holsters. The holsters were empty, because the twin laser pistols were in her hands and aimed down at Starbuck.

He stood in the deep pit he'd fallen into. He'd discovered, before the appearance of the two-gun blonde, that he could not reach the rim by jumping for it.

"Excuse me for blundering into your animal snare, miss," he said up at the girl. "If you'll give me a hand getting out, why, I'll be happy to help you replace all the branches, leaves and twigs back over the top. Then, when a real wild beast comes strolling by, he'll never know that—"

"Do you like to hear yourself babbling, jerko?"

"Sure, but—"

"Well, I sure as hell don't."

Starbuck scrutinized her. "You know, I sense a distinct lack of sympathy with my plight."

"We dug the damn hole for you, jerko."

"Gee, I'm touched. All this work just for me."

"We got some old 'bots who do it."

"How'd you know I was coming?"

"She said you might be."

"Robber? You've got her?"

The girl laughed. It wasn't an especially heart-warming laugh. "Same like we got you," she told him and spit into the pit.

He dodged, brushing against a black dirt wall and causing a fat wiggling orange worm to come falling free. "You folks planning to keep me down here or—"

"I'm going to signal Psycho in a minute. He'll come get you."

"Psycho? He doesn't sound like much fun."

"Aw, sure, he is. You're going to have lots of good times with him," she promised. "Just like Robber is."

Starbuck clenched his fists and kept himself from saying something strong and angry to her. "Can't wait until . . ."

"Wait until what, jerko?"

"Oh, until I meet Psycho."

Starbuck had been distracted by a silent figure that was sneaking up behind the unsuspecting blonde. A figure that was extending an odd metal arm toward her from behind.

CHAPTER ELEVEN

The lean blonde, despite Starbuck's best efforts to distract her, finally sensed she was being stalked. She started to turn around, guns swinging up.

But the metal arm gave off a sudden harsh humming and a thin beam of purplish light shot out of the pointing forefinger.

"Damn you, Scrap—" She said only that before she stiffened, tottered backwards and dropped down into Starbuck's pit.

He sort of caught her.

When he got up from the broken branches and dirt, the blonde was stretched out on the ground and both her guns were his.

"Don't be frettin' none," said the sandy-haired young man standing at the rim of the pit. "Candy's nothin' but stunned."

"Yep, I noticed," said Starbuck, eyeing the fellow

and his coppery right arm. "What I'm more interested in at the moment, though, is the status of our relationship."

"Heck, we're friends."

"I'd hate to have to use these guns of hers."

"Shucks, I realize you got no way of knowin' if I'm trustworthy or not. But I am." From inside his loose-fitting tan jacket he produced a coil of rope. "Name's Scrapper. You?"

"Starbuck." He caught the end of the rope that Scrapper lowered to him. "You sure you can tug me up out of—"

"I'm a lot stronger than I look, Starbuck. No kiddin'."

He was, and Starbuck was soon up on the forest floor. "Much obliged," he said.

"Listen now," said Scrapper as he reeled in his rope. "I ain't exactly bein' just altruistic in this here business, you see. Not that me and Psycho's bunch ain't natural born enemies and all. Thing is, see, I couldn't help overhearin' your conversation with Candy."

"Glad you did."

Scratching at his sharp nose with a metal forefinger, Scrapper said, "They got Robber and you're aimin' to save her. Ain't that about the situation?"

Starbuck glanced up at the fog-shrouded treetops. "Just about," he replied.

"Wellsir now, Robber's sort of a special friend of mine," he explained. "I like her, she likes me. Even though everybody else over in her enclave don't much cotton to me. I'm a loner, don't like livin' too close to anybody. And there's my arm, too."

"Looks like a darn exceptional arm to me."

Grinning, Scrapper rubbed at the metal arm with the fingers of his flesh and blood hand. "Built the whole dang thing myself, designed it, too. It can do all sorts of interestin' stuff," he said proudly. "Made it from scrap of this and that. I scrounged parts from all over the planetoid. You'd be surprised at all that was left behind when them Skyfarms folks pulled up stakes long time back."

"I've bumped into some of what they left," said Starbuck. "How'd you come to lose your real arm?"

Scrapper shook his head. "Never had but one," he answered. "Born this way. You could call me a mutant or, like most do, a freak."

Starbuck asked him, "You got any idea where they're holding Robber?"

"A pretty darn good one, yep. Would you care to team up and rescue her?"

"Sounds like a good idea."

"Partners then." Scrapper held out his metal hand.

Starbuck shook it. "Partners."

The fat one had a knife. He sat in the sagging sling chair, watching Robber. He was an immense young man in a suit of work clothes that didn't exactly fit him. The buttons and the other fastenings were straining. "I like you," he repeated, rubbing at the knife blade with a fat thumb. "Truly I do, Robber."

The young woman sat on the floor of this single-room shack, hands tied behind her. She said nothing.

"I had to cut you some when we caught you," continued the fat young man, his body jiggling. "But I didn't hurt you all that badly, did I?"

She looked away from him, at the small cracked window in the wall. The mist pressed against it, seeping in through the zigzag crack. The odor of the stagnant pond outside came in, too.

"You have to understand," continued the fat young man, "that you and I are on opposite sides. This is *our* territory, so when *you* try to cross it, we naturally have to stop you. We have to hurt you, too, make an example of you. Otherwise your people would think they can just—"

"Shut up, Threetime," said the other occupant of the shack. He was not tall, only about five foot four. He had a chalky white look to him. His closecut blond hair was pale, faded looking. He was watching at the room's other window.

"Pleasant conversation relieves the monotony, Psycho. Makes the time pass much—"

"Didn't I just tell you to shut the hell up?"

Threetime nodded, chins wobbling. "If you want my opinion, you're worrying needlessly. Candy will certainly—"

"No more talk." Psycho gestured impatiently with his laser pistol.

When Threetime gave a resigned shrug, his whole body quivered.

Psycho glanced at Robber. "Tell me some more about this guy who's following you."

She said, "I don't know anything more. I'm not even sure he is following me."

Psycho checked the window again. "Candy's taking too damn long. If she spotted the guy, she ought—"

"We don't know how far behind he is," reminded Threetime.

"Yeah, but I told her to watch a while and then, if nobody showed, to come back and report."

"She's not the most reliable of people."

"Shut up," suggested Psycho.

The fat young man returned his attention to Robber. "As I was saying, you and I could be friends," he said. "All you have to do is abandon that bunch you reside with and—"

"Quiet," said Psycho.

"I was merely—"

"I think I hear something." The pale Psycho was close to the window, listening and watching. "Something's coming this way. Somebody."

"Probably Candy."

"No, this is somebody heavier, noisier."

"She isn't exactly lightfooted."

Psycho said, "I can...damn."

"What?" Curious, the immense Threetime started to grunt up out of his chair.

"Saw somebody," said Psycho, eyes narrowed, watching the misty woodlands outside the shack. "Coming through the swamp. Looked like...hell, some sort of robot."

"That's very unlikely. None of those old mechs work well enough to—"

"It was big, one of those farmhand 'bots. Had a scythe for a right hand."

"Why would a thing like that, granted there's even one in working order on the whole damn planetoid, be coming to call on us?"

Psycho nodded at the fat young man. "Go find out. It's out there in the swamp, in the trees about three, four hundred yards off."

"The mist is making you see things that aren't—"

"Go find out what the hell it's doing there," ordered Psycho. "Take the laser rifle."

Sighing loudly, Threetime put his knife away in

its sheath. "We could simply wait until it—"

"Get moving."

The shack's wooden floor creaked as Threetime lumbered over to take up the rifle that was leaning against the wall. "If this is your imagination, I'm really—"

"Go see." He reached out, opened the door. Mist came spilling in.

Sighing again, the fat young man ventured out into the fog.

CHAPTER TWELVE

In the throne room of a Cylon base ship the helmeted Imperious Leader sat upon his multifaceted pedestal. The shifting light in the vast, dim chamber made the surface of the pedestal flash and gleam in a distracting way.

The metal-faced Centurion who approached the pedestal reflected the jagged flashes of light. "Permission to speak," he requested, bowing slightly at the bulky figure above him.

"Granted. Proceed." Most of the Leader's head was lost in shadows.

"We have monitored an undecipherable transmission from the Hohne System."

"What do you mean undecipherable? There is no problem the Cylon mind cannot solve."

"I meant to say *as yet* undecipherable."

"Continue, and take care to be more precise."

"The signal was being sent to the planet Aeries."

"By the Colonial Fleet?"

"We believe so."

"I see," said the Leader. "Whoever is sending the signal doesn't know we have long since destroyed the colonies on Aeries. Dispatch a patrol to destroy whatever humanoids are to be found out there in the Hohne System."

"By your command," said the Centurion.

Psycho hunched his shoulders, shook his head from side to side. "What the hell is going on?"

Moving away from the window, he crossed over to Robber.

"I asked you a question," he said. "What's happening out there? Why hasn't Threetime come back?"

"I don't know."

He squatted, scowling at her. "First Candy, now Threetime," he said. "Are some of your people out there?"

"No," said Robber. "You know damn well I'm miles from my home territory."

"You're here. They could be, too."

"I'm here because the ship I was flying went on the fritz," she said. "You already made me tell you all about that."

Psycho took hold of her jaw in his hand. "Who is it then? This guy that's trailing you?"

"How the hell should I know?"

Holding her head immobile, he slapped her with his other hand. Three times, hard. "What's going on out there? Tell me!"

"I don't know."

"Listen, I don't want to have to cut you up anymore," Psycho told her in a low, calm voice. "But if you don't—"

Someone knocked on the door of the shack.

Jerking to his feet, Psycho spun to face the door.

The knocking was repeated. Louder and firmer.

Psycho drew his lasergun. "Who's out there?"

Whoever it was didn't respond. The knocking sounded again.

"Threetime? Is that you?"

More knocking.

"Candy?"

Knocking.

"All right, you bastard!"

Psycho fired straight at the door, his gun crackling and humming. The top half of the wooden door vanished. Nothing showed in the gap except the misty swampland outside.

Psycho took three cautious steps closer to the doorway.

A big metal-bodied robot rolled into view from beside the door. "Howdy," he said, waving his scythe hand in greeting.

"What are you doing here? What do you want?"

"Howdy."

"Get the hell away from here or—"

A door-sized chunk of the rear wall suddenly disintegrated. "Nothing like a robot to create a diversion," said Scrapper, stepping through the hole.

"So you're the freak who—"

Scrapper stunned him at that point, using the beam built into his forefinger.

Psycho fell to the floor.

Starbuck entered by way of the front door. "I knew we'd meet again," he said to Robber as he hurried over to her. Kneeling, he cut her bonds.

As best she could with numbed arms she hugged him. "Thanks," she said. "I'm sorry I beaned you."

Scrapper nodded to himself. "Ain't that the way it always goes," he observed. "I do most of the rough work and somebody else gets the gratitude."

CHAPTER THIRTEEN

"This must've been quite a setup back when," said Captain Apollo.

"Business seems to've slumped off lately," commented Boomer.

They were crossing vast, overgrown fields, heading for a cluster of abandoned buildings.

"No way of telling," said Apollo, "how long this has been deserted."

"I'd guess a good while," said the lieutenant. "One thing about being associated with Starbuck, you get to see some interesting places"

"And meet some interesting women."

"Yeah, I'm kind of anxious to see this current lady he's tangled up with. What was her name, Robber?"

"According to the reliable Cora, yes."

They slowed their pace as they neared the Skyfarms, Ltd. buildings.

"Robber," repeated Boomer. "She sounds like a tough lady."

"She'd have to be to get the best of Starbuck. He usually . . . hey, there's somebody in front of that warehouse." Apollo drew his laser pistol.

"Only a robot," said Boomer. "Doesn't look to be functioning."

"We'll approach with caution anyway."

The overalled mechanical man was slumped in his chair. "Howdy . . ." he croaked when they were a few yards from him.

"It's just barely working," said Boomer.

Apollo was at the entrance to the empty warehouse. "Somebody's been in here." He entered.

Lieutenant Boomer followed. "Over there," he said, pointing. "Some kind of fracas. Yeah, look at all the footprints in the dust. It doesn't look like a friendly encounter."

Crouching, Apollo touched at a dark spot on the wood flooring. "This is blood," he said.

"Not much of it around, though."

"Meaning somebody was hurt but not killed."

"If Starbuck was here, he's moved on. So we—"

"You inside there!" boomed a voice from outside. "Throw down your weapons and come out. Quick!"

"Wasn't all that difficult," Scrapper was explaining as they made their way through the misty swampland. "Just a matter of rigging one of them old farmbots to do a few simple chores."

"Scrap's a wizard with gadgets," added Starbuck. He was at the head of the line, with Robber just behind him. "He got that mechanical fieldhand to walk and talk just great."

"Then we used him to decoy Threetime out of that there shack," said Scrapper. "After we had the fat boy safely stunned, then we up and sent the 'bot to rap on the shack door. While poor old Psycho was givin' all his attention to that, I snuck around back. After peeking through the window to make sure where you was, I just up and dropped in, usin' this finger here to cut me an entry."

Robber smiled back at him over her shoulder. "I appreciate what you did," she said. "You, too, Starbuck."

The lieutenant added cigar smoke to the swirling mist. "I happen to be what is called chivalrous," he told her. "That means I am compelled to help maidens in distress."

"Of course," reminded the dark-haired young woman, "I wouldn't have been in most of this trouble if that nitwit computer of yours hadn't futzed the Viper and forced me to land such a damn long way from—"

"Hey, my computer was just doing her duty," Starbuck said. "You, dear Robber, had highjacked my ship . . . which in some of the more civilized corners of the universe might be construed as piracy. . . . To continue, you swiped my ship, left me for dead—"

"Hell, I only borrowed your dippy ship because mine was flooey," she said. "And you sure weren't anywhere near dead when—"

"Might be," put in Scrapper, "a good idea if you explained why you was so anxious to get away from that there asteroid, Robber."

"That's obvious," she said impatiently. "Croad was on my tail."

"Him I met," said Starbuck. "He's the local law. That makes you, my love, the local outlaw, since he was—"

"Ain't exactly that simple," said Scrapper. "Them

enforcers say they're the law, but...well, they run the prison colony on Proteus. And that ain't the most honest and upright place you could wish for."

"It's a sinkhole," commented Robber.

"She grew up there," said Scrapper, "but was lucky enough to escape and get over here."

"That was when I was seventeen," she said. "For the past year or so I've lived with a group of other escapees, south of here. We farm, and raise cattle."

"And where does the Ambrosa come in?"

"There's a lot of that on Proteus," she replied. "And there are ways of picking up a cargo now and then. Risky, but worth trying. This time Croad nearly caught me."

"He nearly caught me, too," said Starbuck. "In fact, I borrowed his fighter to come here."

Robber laughed. "Seems to me that makes you an outlaw, too."

"Well, it could be that in these parts that's the best thing to be." He puffed on his cigar.

Scrapper said, "We want to go off on the trail that branches off this one just ahead. From what you tell me, Starbuck, it's a shortcut to where the fighter and your ship are."

"You don't have to fly me back to my group," the girl said to Starbuck. "I can manage it on foot."

"Nope," he told her. "When I go out on a date with a lady, I always see her safely home."

CHAPTER FOURTEEN

Boomer had his eye to a crack in the warehouse wall. "Seems like there's just one man out there," he said quietly. "The lasergun he's toting looks old-fashioned but effective."

"I'll surrender to him," said Apollo. "Give me a little time, then distract him." Boomer nodded.

Apollo walked to the doorway, tossed out his pistol. "Okay," he called, "I'm coming out."

Hands high, he marched into the weedy field.

The man with the gun was some two hundred feet away. Tall, thickset, he wore brown clothes. There was a star emblem on his jacket.

"I want your partner, too," he told Apollo.

The captain feigned surprise, kept moving toward him. "What partner?"

"The black guy who went into the damn warehouse with you."

Smiling, Apollo said, "I don't like to argue with

77

a fellow who packs a gun, but I didn't go into that place with—"

"Look, if he doesn't come out in another minute, I'll gun you down."

Apollo was only a few feet away from the thickset lawman now. "Who exactly are you?" he asked him.

"I'm an enforcer," he answered.

"Then we're on the same side." Apollo started lowering his hands. "Because I—"

"Keep 'em up."

"Sure, okay. But the point is, we're probably looking for the same man," continued Apollo. "He's a middle-sized young fellow, with hair the color of straw. He smokes foul cigars and dotes on stealing other people's means of transportation."

The lawman studied Apollo's face. "Well, as a matter of fact, that does sound like him," he said. "I never laid eyes on the little bastard myself, but—"

"You can be thankful you didn't." Apollo edged nearer. "He's a vile criminal, notorious for his—"

"What the devil?"

Over by the warehouse doorway the lounging robot had suddenly stood up and begun waving his arms.

The husky lawman's attention was drawn to that.

Apollo lunged and caught the enforcer's arm. He twisted the gun from his grasp. Then Apollo jabbed him twice in the midsection and once in the jaw. When the man hit the ground he was unconscious.

"Starbuck's a bad influence," remarked Apollo. "Now I'm knocking out minions of the law."

Scrapper said, "We might as well be on the safe side, folks."

They'd halted by a small forest pond.

"We're mighty near to your ships," the young man said, pointing toward the trees with his metal hand. "Won't take me no time at all to make sure there ain't no more of Psycho's people, or anyone else waitin' 'round. And goin' alone I can move as quiet and silent as the breeze."

Snuffing out his cigar on the mossy ground, Starbuck seated himself on a hollow log. "Good idea, Scrap," he said. "You go on and get the lay of the land. We'll wait here."

Grinning, Scrapper moved away into the shadows between the high trees.

"Feeling cowardly, Starbuck?" inquired Robber, leaning against the bole of a broad tree.

"Merely cautious, love," he said. "Since first I paid a visit to your fair galaxy I've been conked on the head, highjacked, abandoned and dropped in a pit. Experiences like that make one a bit wary."

The young woman nodded, smiled a crooked smile. "Sure."

"If a fellow," said the lieutenant after a moment, "wanted to address you by your real name instead of your desperado handle, what would he call you?"

She answered, "I don't have any other name."

"How's that?"

"It has to do with the prison."

"But you must've had another name before you got sent there."

"I was born there."

"Huh?" He stood up.

Robber shook her head. "I'm not all that anxious to talk about it."

"You lived all your life on this Proteus? I don't see—"

"There's no reason why you have to," she told him. "Chance brought us together, chance'll separate us again. That's the way life is, not anything to get serious about."

"You're pretty cynical for a youngster," he observed.

"I haven't been a youngster for a long time," she said, glancing in the direction Scrapper had gone. "What about you, Starbuck? Who are you?"

"Well . . ." He poked his boot toe into the mossy ground.

"Like to ask questions, but not answer them, huh?"

"I'm a warrior."

"What does that mean?"

He pointed upward. "Well, in my case, love, it means I'm stationed on an enormous spaceship called a battlestar," he answered. "Right now I'm supposed to be exploring your quaint galaxy here. Without bragging, Robber, I've got to tell you that I am usually darn good at my job. Flying a Viper, exploring, fighting. I excell at all that." He shrugged. "But, to be perfectly honest, ever since I met you on that halfwit asteroid I've been fouling up."

She smiled. "I can see you're going to use me as an excuse when you get home to your battlestar," she said. "'I met this vicious woman outlaw, sir, and she led me astray.'"

"I've been leading myself astray," Starbuck said. "When I heard you might be in trouble, I had to come after you."

"Must be my charm."

He eyed her. "That really, you know, could be the reason," he said. "Because if you look at this logically—"

"We got us a mite of a problem," said Scrapper as he silently returned to them.

"What's wrong?" asked the lieutenant.

"Well," began Scrapper, rubbing at his metal arm, "that clearing yonder's sort of more crowded than you described it."

"How so?"

"First off, there's two more ships like yours. They—"

"Must be from the *Galactica*," said Starbuck, brightening. "Could be Apollo and Boomer, or Jolly and—"

"What else?" asked Robber.

"Another enforcer fighter," answered Scrapper.

Frowning, Starbuck said, "Where are the people who go with all this aircraft?"

Scrapper shook his head. "Didn't see hide nor hair of 'em," he said. "I didn't go up close to none of them ships, mind you, but it sure looks like there wasn't anybody around."

"Seems likely that Apollo and Boomer are off looking for me," reflected Starbuck. "And the occupants of the enforcer ship are, too."

"They want me," said Robber.

"Okay," said Starbuck. "You two wait for me here. I'm going to the clearing and see if I can talk to Cora. She's my computer. She ought to know where my buddies are. I'll get together with them and then swing back here for you."

"That's risky," said Robber.

"I know." He grinned. "But I'm awful anxious to prove to you that I'm not a coward."

• • •

Crouched amidst brush, Starbuck scanned the clearing.

Sure enough, there was an additional fighter and two more Vipers.

"Looks like Apollo and Boomer came hunting for me when I got myself sidetracked," he said to himself.

No one was in the area with the ships now, as far as Starbuck could tell.

He remained where he was, watching and listening. Soon he'd approach his own Viper. It stood to reason Apollo or Boomer had talked to his computer. Cora might know just where they—

The barrel of a laser pistol poked against his spine. "Nice seeing you again," said Croad.

CHAPTER FIFTEEN

Boomer narrowed his eyes. "I don't like the look of this next stretch of country," he said as they approached misty woodlands.

"We're not on a sightseeing tour, old buddy," said Apollo. "Starbuck came this way."

"'Least he's still on his own two feet."

"The footprints indicate that, yep. He's following somebody who's carrying something fairly heavy," said the captain as they moved along the trail.

"The body of Starbuck's ladyfriend maybe?"

"That's sure a possibility."

"You don't have to worry about that, gents. He's alive and well." A lanky young man with a metal arm appeared out of the mist a few yards directly ahead of them.

"Who are you?" Apollo's hand hovered over his holster.

"Name's Scrapper," he answered. "Suppose you tell me your names. I got a good reason for asking."

"I'm Apollo, and this is Boomer."

"Good, I was hoping you'd say that." Scrapper grinned. "You're friends of Starbuck."

"We are, but how do you—"

"Robber," Scrapper called. "It's okay, come on over."

A slim dark-haired young woman joined them.

Boomer asked, "Is she the one who started all this mess?"

"Starbuck brought most of it on himself," said Robber. "But we haven't got time to argue. Croad's got him."

"Croad?" said Apollo.

"The situation is this," said Scrapper. "We was goin' back to where your ships are, on account of Starbuck was aimin' to give Robber a lift home. Except there was more ships than anticipated and he decided to go in alone, check out the situation with Cora. His computer, you know."

Boomer said, "So what happened?"

"Wellsir, we waited a spell for him," said Scrapper, "and he never came back. So I took me another look."

Robber said, "Scrapper got there just in time to see Croad hustle Starbuck into his fighter ship and take off."

"Had I got there just a mite sooner," said Scrapper sadly, "I could've stunned Croad, kept him from carting Starbuck off like that." He tapped the metal finger he used for stunning.

Apollo asked, "Where's this Croad likely to take him?"

"To Proteus," said Robber. "To the prison."

• • •

"Don't you think," Starbuck had suggested as the fighter lifted off, "that we ought to wait for your friends?"

"What friends?" said Croad.

"The fellows in the other fighter. You didn't come alone, did—"

"Yauk can take care of himself," the lean enforcer said as he worked the controls of the ship. "He'll run Robber to the ground and haul her in."

"I don't mind going back and waiting," said the lieutenant amiably. "Not at all."

"Just shut up."

The ship went climbing away from the surface of the planetoid.

Starbuck inquired, "Mind if I smoke?"

"If you can do it with your hands manacled behind you like that," said Croad, "go ahead."

"Well, I was hoping you'd unshackle me."

"Not a chance."

Starbuck shifted into a slightly less uncomfortable position in the seat he'd been dumped into. "Why do you want Robber?"

"Same reason we want you," answered Croad. "Smuggling. In your case, of course, there's also assault, theft and a whole nice stewpot of other charges."

"Maybe I'd better explain who I really am."

"I know who you are, pal."

"Nope, actually, you only think you do. See, I come from a spacecraft that's—"

"Save it," advised Croad.

"But if I explain the situation to you now, you can just release me. That way there's no need of a trial or—" Starbuck fell silent as Croad began to laugh.

"A trial!" Croad said. "A trial!"

Long ago it had been a thriving spaceport. Now the jungle had moved back, reclaiming the fields, the silos, the buildings and warehouses. Except for a small area that was still used for landings and takeoffs, weeds and high grass were everywhere. And crates. They overflowed the weatherbeaten warehouses and were stacked high in the weedy fields.

"Welcome to Proteus," said Croad as the fighter set down.

"Not the jolliest spot I've ever been," said Starbuck.

Croad chuckled. "You'll get used to it," he assured him, unbuckling from his seat.

"Look, you really better take me to whoever's running this whole show. Because otherwise—"

"Starbuck," said the enforcer evenly, "you'll get along a lot better here on Proteus if you quit bitching."

"I'm just trying to save you trouble, because before too long some of my—"

"Can you get your butt out of that seat and walk on out of this ship?" Croad opened the cabin door.

"Sure, except—"

"Then do it."

Starbuck obliged, following the lawman out of the fighter.

Waiting outside was another lawman, holding a laser rifle. "This the one, Croad?"

"Yeah, he's the wise bastard who stole my ship."

"I see you got it back."

"Always get back what's mine."

Starbuck, hands chained behind his back, was

looking around. The cases were stacked up everywhere. "Those crates look sort of familiar," he remarked.

"Like the ones you were smuggling, pal," said Croad.

"You mean there's Ambrosa in all these?" Starbuck was impressed. "Hey, that's got to be worth—"

"Not worth a damn thing to you," said Croad. "You walk over to that grey building yonder. We'll fix you up with a nice cell."

CHAPTER SIXTEEN

His cell was airy but not roomy. Three of the walls were of grey stone; the fourth was steel bars and door. The furnishings were a lumpy cot and basic toilet facilities. Across the dimly lit corridor Starbuck could see three similar cells. Each was occupied.

Directly opposite him was a large, broad-shouldered man. "What's your name?" he asked, stroking his shaggy beard.

"Starbuck," he answered.

The bearded man frowned. "Starbuck? That's a new one on me," he admitted. He held up a bottle of Ambrosa, toasting. "Well, here's to our new mate, Starbuck. Whatever the hell that is."

There was a plump blonde woman of thirty on the bearded man's left, and a small, stoop-shouldered man of sixty in the cell to his right. They, too, drank a toast from bottles of Ambrosa.

"Drink up, lad," urged the bearded prisoner.

Starbuck noticed the full bottle of Ambrosa sitting on the stone floor beside his cot. "Thanks, but I'm not exactly in the mood for—"

"Are you too good to drink with us?" asked the blonde.

"Nope, not at all, folks." He picked up the bottle, pretended to take a long swig.

Nodding approvingly, the bearded man said, "Welcome to Proteus Prison, lad. I'm Assault Nine. The lady next door is Adulteress Fourteen. And this shifty-eyed old wretch is Forger Six. You can't trust him a bit."

"Is that fair?" protested the older man. "Give the lad a chance to make up his own mind." He smiled a crooked smile. "In the weeks and months ahead, Starbuck, you'll come to appreciate me for my true worth."

"Actually I'm not planning to stay that long."

Assault laughed a chesty laugh. "You don't have much say in the matter."

"Well, soon as I can explain to someone in authority who I really am, why—"

"I wonder," said the blonde, "if our original sinners were as ignorant and naive as this one."

"Original sinners?" said Starbuck.

"She refers to our ancestors," explained Assault. "The ones who were first sentenced here long ago."

Starbuck blinked. "You mean to tell me all you folks are doing time for crimes your ancestors committed?"

Forger said, "That's better than being an original sinner like you, Starbuck."

"What exactly is starbucking?" asked Adulteress,

moving close to the bars. "If you told us, we might—"

"It's not an offense. It's just a name, my name," he said, somewhat annoyed. "See, folks, I'm not a criminal at all."

"Lad, it's no use protesting to us," said Assault. "Croad's made up his mind you're to be here and that's it."

"You mean Croad's in charge of this whole prison operation?"

"That he is," said Forger.

"Then I really am in a pickle," said Starbuck.

Assault said, "You've been outside. You must have news of the war."

"The war?"

"Between the colonies and the Alliance," said Assault.

"But the war took place a long—"

"We supply Ambrosa for the Colonial Warriors," said Forger, pride in his voice.

"We may be prisoners," added Adulteress, "yet we're as patriotic as any colonist."

Starbuck went over and sat on his cot. "Getting out of here is going to take a lot more explaining than I figured," he said.

Apollo paced the clearing. "What I'm suggesting to you is the simplest way of doing things," he said.

"Go to hell," said the enforcer.

His name was Yauk and he was the man Apollo had knocked out at the abandoned warehouse. Boomer and Scrapper had brought him back to the ships.

Apollo halted in front of him. "Look, friend, we're both more or less on the same side," he said, impatience showing in his voice. "You escort us to Croad on Proteus and we can arrange—"

"You can *say* any damn thing," the enforcer told them, "but you still might be Cylon agents. And I'll tell you something. This buddy of yours, this Starbuck guy, he tried to kill Croad—and stole his fighter. You two bastards worked me over. Hell, that's not my idea of being on the same side."

"Those," said Boomer, "were just misunderstandings."

"The hell with all of you."

Robber said, "Croad left you behind to find me and bring me in, didn't he?"

"Yeah, and eventually I will."

Nodding, the dark-haired woman turned to Apollo. "You can fly that fighter of his, can't you?"

"Sure."

"Okay, then let's quit wasting time with this idiot," she said. "You'll fly it to Proteus with me as your passenger. If you wear Yauk's outfit, we can land safely at the prison and get inside before they know what's up."

"You won't fool Croad with a dumb stunt like that," said Yauk scornfully.

"It might work," said Apollo thoughtfully.

"Sure," said Scrapper, "and Boomer and me can land nearby. You take out the guards, we'll come scooting in. Heck, the four of us can take over the whole shebang. Easy as pie."

"They'll wipe you out," predicted the enforcer.

"We'll try it," said Apollo.

CHAPTER SEVENTEEN

They hadn't taken Starbuck's cigars away from him. He lit one as he paced his small cell.

Apollo and Boomer were out there somewhere, searching for him. So if he could just relax and wait, they'd eventually track him to the Proteus prison.

Trouble was, Starbuck wasn't the patient type. Being in a cage made him edgy. Puffing on his stogie, he leaned back against the metal bars of his cell door.

The door swung open with a raspy squeak.

"What the heck is this?" he said as he stumbled into the corridor.

"Get back inside," called Assault anxiously. "Close your door, mate."

"They don't like us to do that," said Adulteress, frowning through her bars at him.

Starbuck remained in the stone corridor. "Now, folks," he said, glancing around at his fellow prisoners, "you can't mean that none of these cells are locked."

"They haven't worked in generations," answered Assault, his eyes on the floor. "Central control mechanism went bad ages ago."

Dropping his cigar, a bewildered Starbuck ground it out with his boot heel. "Let me get this straight in my poor old battered brain," he said. "Your cells aren't locked, not a one of 'em, but you all stay here anyway. Why the heck, if you don't mind my asking, do you do that?"

"Tradition," answered Forger.

"It's the way things are," added Assault.

"Our fathers were prisoners," explained Adulteress. "Our mothers were prisoners. And we are prisoners. That's the way things work."

"Hooey." Starbuck fished out another cigar. "Stop acting like nitwits. We're all human beings. And, in case you haven't heard, we have certain rights. The right to freedom is one of 'em. Freedom means you don't mope around in a cell if you can get—"

"That'll be enough out of you, Starbuck." Croad had appeared in the corridor. He glared at Starbuck. "Get the hell back behind bars."

"No. It's going to take you and a couple of your stooges to get me in there again," Starbuck informed the enforcer. "Boy, you've got some deal going here. Keep these poor folks slaving away for nothing while you lord it over them like—"

"There is a purpose to this," cut in Croad. "They produce Ambrosa for the Colonial Warriors, for our fighting men. That's their duty, just as it's ours to enforce the rules. My father was an enforcer and his father—"

"Yeah, sure," said Starbuck impatiently. "But the Colonies long ago forgot about these penal asteroids. They probably think you were wiped out ages ago."

"That's not true," insisted the enforcer. "They don't contact us as frequently as they once did, but—"

"Frequently? Man, you've got Ambrosa piled up to the skies out on those loading docks." Starbuck pointed at the doorway out. "Some of those darn crates have vines growing over 'em. C'mon, admit it."

"That's a lie," said Croad, moving nearer to him. "Now I want you back inside your—"

"Tell us," said Starbuck, facing him, "the last time a Colonial freighter docked here."

"The business of the enforcers is covered by security restrictions. I couldn't possibly—"

"Have you ever seen a freighter, Croad? Did your father?"

"Get into your cell."

"That's not much of an answer." Starbuck turned to Assault. "You people have been wasting your darn lives. You haven't helped the Colonies."

Assault looked at the enforcer. "Is what he's saying true?"

"No, none of it," Croad assured him. "You wouldn't take the word of a—"

"You don't have to take anybody's word," said Starbuck. "All you have to do is walk out of that cell, Assault, and go outside. Look at the darn docking area and the spaceport. Then you tell me if this whole mess here isn't just a stupid boondoggle to keep the enforcers in power."

"I'm warning you, Starbuck," said Croad, reaching for his lasergun. "If you don't—"

"Wait," said Assault.

"There's no need to pay any attention to Starbuck," said the enforcer.

Ignoring him, Assault opened the door of his cell.

Robber tapped her fingertips on the side of her seat. "You've known Starbuck for a while, huh?"

"I sure have." Apollo, dressed now in the clothes of the enforcer, was at the controls of the fighter. They were nearing Proteus. "Can you give me a landing pattern that'll set us now by the prison?"

Nodding, she reached over, punched out one on the dash controls. "That'll do it."

"Much obliged."

Robber said, "I find I have mixed feelings about him."

"Starbuck? He takes getting used to," Apollo told her. "What it comes down to finally is...Starbuck is Starbuck."

"I realize that," she said. "When I...um... incapacitated him and took his Viper, I thought I'd never see him again." She shrugged.

The dark asteroid grew larger and larger beyond the window of the ship.

"For many folks Starbuck is like a bad habit. Hard to give up."

"The reason I wanted the Viper originally," Robber said as they began to descend, "was to try to get to Aeries. My old shuttle'd never make that jaunt. I have relatives there—"

"When's the last time you were in touch with them?"

"I've never been in touch," the dark-haired girl replied. "But my mother told me about her people being there. And when I was a kid, she taught me a merchant's code to use to communicate with—"

"Hold it," said Apollo. "Did you use that code to try and contact Aeries while you were in the Viper?"

"Yes."

"The Cylons conquered that planet quite some time ago," he said. "If they picked up your transmission, they'll be sending somebody to see who sent it."

Robber folded her hands in her lap. "I didn't know," she said. "I'm sorry."

"You couldn't have known, isolated as you are," said Apollo. "But we can almost certainly expect a Cylon visit. And their visits are never friendly ones."

"That's something to worry about," said Robber. "But let's get Starbuck free first."

"Let's," agreed Apollo.

Boomer sniffed at the air. "That smell's familiar," he said, "but I can't quite place—"

"Ambrosa," said Scrapper. "From the distilleries yonder."

They had landed on Proteus and were moving through a wooded area toward the rear of the prison complex.

"They make the stuff here?"

"It's just about the sole industry, Boomer."

"In our part of the universe Ambrosa's damn rare."

"Not on Proteus," he said. "They're up to here in the dang stuff, which is why Robber and a few others run loads over to the other asteroids and planetoids now and then."

The lieutenant asked, "Are the distilleries part of the prison?"

"Right behind it," he answered. "You'll see the whole shootin' match in about...oops. Hold up." Scrapper held his metal hand in front of Boomer to halt his progress along the pathway.

"Something wrong?"

"Heard somethin' off that way and...oh... greetin's, Hustler."

A small, bearded old man stood, barely visible, in among the trees. He leaned on a knobby wooden staff. "Wellsir, if it ain't Scrapper himself," he said in a quavery voice. "You come for a load?"

"Nope, nope, just a friendly visit."

"'Cause we been able to acquire another hundred cases."

"I'll tell Robber."

"Aw, she took her last load from Lightfingers and his bunch." Hustler shook his head sadly, causing his long beard to flutter. "Any fool knows he waters his Ambrosa. It ain't got the quality ours has."

Scrapper inquired, "How you been?"

"Can't complain," answered Hustler. "The terrible pain in my back ain't no better but I've learned to live with it. The dizzy spells been a mite better. And the last time I fell over in a swoon I landed on mossy ground and didn't break anything. So all in all, when you ask how I been, Scrapper, I got to say—"

"Well, it's been right nice chattin' with you," Scrapper said, grinning. "We'll be moseyin' on now. And if you hear a lot of loud noises in a spell, don't pay that no mind."

"Way my hearing is these days, I'm lucky to hear anything at all." He gave them a wave before disappearing among the trees.

"That's one of the dangerous side effects of smugglin'," said Scrapper as he and Boomer continued on their way to the prison. "You get to samplin' too much of the stuff yourself."

CHAPTER EIGHTEEN

Commander Adama sat in a comfortable chair in his quarters, a pile of reports on his lap. He leaned back in the chair, eyes nearly shut.

"Colonel Tigh requests permission to enter," said a talkbox overhead.

"Granted." Sitting up, Adama moved the stack of papers to a nearby tabletop.

The black colonel looked worried as he came into the room. "Those signals that were sent out to Aeries," he began.

"Have produced results?"

"Not the sort I'd have wished for, but results, yes," answered Tigh. "Our long-range scanners indicate three Cylon fighters have entered the asteroid dust cloud."

"Do they appear to be heading for the *Galactica?*"

"No. The scanners indicate that their projected

course is to the area from which Starbuck's Recon Viper One sent the signals," said Colonel Tigh. "That's where Apollo and Boomer are, too."

Adama stroked his chin. "The Cylons must be scanning on a narrow beam," he said. "Or they'd have picked us up by now."

"Eventually they will spot us."

"We'll have to bring the fleet to flank speed," decided the commander. "Then set a new course to put as much space between us and those Cylons as possible."

"In that case Apollo's patrol may not be able to find us."

"We won't change course immediately," said Adama. "But if there's no sign of Apollo and the others soon, we'll have to act."

"Yes, sir," said Tigh without much enthusiasm.

Croad lost his lasergun in the scuffle.

The prisoners came rushing free of their cells, heading for the outside. Starbuck was at the forefront, leading the excited procession.

"Fresh air," said Assault when he reached the docking area. "All these years, moving from the prison cells to the distilleries, we rarely got outside."

"That's one of the things freedom's about," Starbuck pointed out. "Being able to breathe fresh air when you want...excuse me." He aimed the gun he'd acquired from Croad at the approaching enforcer. "Drop that laser rifle, my lad."

"What the hell is going—"

"This is what you call," explained the lieutenant, "a prison break."

"But these people can't—"

"The rifle. Drop it. Otherwise I may have to render you defunct."

The enforcer dropped his weapon, stood back and watched the dozens of prisoners come pouring out into the light and air.

"I see what you mean about the crates," said Assault, who was walking toward the nearest stack of Ambrosa boxes.

"Years of work," said Adulteress, sighing. "Years and years, all for nothing."

"Not exactly nothing," said Starbuck. "You ought to be able to sell this stuff all across the universe. The profits will be fantastic."

The children of the prisoners were running and laughing, climbing the crates, tumbling in the high grass, making up brand new outdoor games.

Assault shook his head. "There were times," he said, "when I suspected something like this. But I . . . I never tried to find out."

"It's easy to get into a rut," said Starbuck. "The important thing is, it's over now and you folks can start a new kind of life."

"That won't be easy."

"I know."

"But you're right. We have . . . ho! There's an enforcer ship coming in for a landing."

"Nothing to fear," grinned Starbuck, patting his laser gun. "I'll act as a welcoming committee."

"You sure you can bring this off?" Robber had asked as the fighter lowered toward a landing next to the Proteus prison.

"Impersonating an enforcer? Sure," answered Apollo.

"You don't look all that convincing in Yauk's clothes."

Apollo laughed. "I can see why Starbuck likes you," he said. "You're feisty."

"He doesn't like me much."

"Trust me, he . . . hey, what's going on down there?"

Robber leaned forward in her seat. "Prisoners," she said. "They're rushing out of the damn place."

"Is that usual?"

"Not at all."

Apollo concentrated on landing. When that was accomplished, he said, "I think I know what's going on. There's Starbuck."

The lieutenant, gun in hand and cigar in mouth, was strolling over to their ship.

Opening the cabin door, Apollo dropped to the ground. "You shouldn't have gone to all this trouble for us, old boy," he said. "A simple brass band would've sufficed."

"I'll be darned," said Starbuck. "Fancy meeting you here . . . and *you*."

Very tentatively Robber climbed free of the ship. She remained close to it, watching Starbuck.

He thrust his gun in his belt, then hugged her. "I'm glad to see you again."

"Let's not overdo it," she said, slowly pulling free of him. "There's no need to get so damn . . . but, well, I missed you, too."

"See? Didn't I warn you that eventually you'd realize how charming I—"

"Don't let me spoil this reunion," said Apollo. "But

I really think we ought to think about departing."

"Something wrong?" Starbuck asked him.

"It's possible we have Cylons looking for us," said Apollo.

CHAPTER NINETEEN

"Well, shucks," remarked Scrapper, "we didn't get to have us no dang fun at all. Looks like the fightin' is all over and done."

"That's okay by me," Boomer said as they walked over to the others.

"Howdy, Starbuck," said Scrapper, giving him a lazy salute with his metal hand. "Are there maybe some enforcers still holed up inside the prison? Diehards who won't give up without a pitched battle and lots of—"

"They all surrendered, every darn one of 'em, just before you guys arrived," the lieutenant informed him.

"Dang." Scrapper kicked at the high grass.

Starbuck nudged Boomer. "Have you feasted your orbs on all these crates surrounding us? Each and every one contains flasks of *aged* Ambrosa," he explained, grinning. "Now, envision a situation in which you and I, Boomer, return in triumph to the *Galactica* with a few cases of aged Ambrosa tucked beneath our arms. I am already beloved and idolized by all and sundry aboard the ship, but this coup'll—"

"Can we skip the bedtime yarns," suggested Apollo, "and get to the problem at hand?"

Boomer asked, "You worrying about the Cylons?"

Nodding, the captain said, "Signals were sent to Aeries. And since the Cylons control that particular planet, they must've picked them up."

"Who was dumb enough to—"

"Me," Robber told the black lieutenant. "I didn't know that Aeries was no longer friendly."

Starbuck gave her a reassuring pat on the backside. "No use crying over spilled Ambrosa," he advised. "The thing to do now is figure a way to outfox the patrol the Cylons will almost certainly send."

Apollo asked, "Got a notion?"

Starbuck took out one of his vile cigars. He lit it, puffed. "We'll need my new Recon Viper," he said. "And that means returning to the delightful planetoid we just vacated. *And* getting the crate in flying shape again."

"We may not have time for that," said Apollo.

"Let's gamble that we do." Starbuck, unexpectedly, kissed Robber on the cheek. "Don't go away, my love. I'll return to you as soon as the skies are safe for democracy."

"You don't owe me any—"

"Hush," he said. "Just follow instructions and all will be well." Spinning on his heel, he started for the fighter. "Which of you blokes is going to give me a lift?"

Boomer looked at Apollo. "Shall we flip for the honor?"

"I'll take him," volunteered Apollo. "I think I know what he has in mind and . . . well, it just might work."

"I'm impressed," said Boomer.

"At the way I have, both deftly and swiftly, gotten this Recon Viper back into flying shape?" Starbuck shut his tool kit, then wiped his forehead with the back of his hand.

"Nope, at how you manage to charm women in every darn galaxy that we hit," said the lieutenant. "When you and Robber parted, there were tears in her eyes."

"She's just got hayfever." Apollo was looking skyward. "And she's allergic to him."

Wiping his palms on his backside, Starbuck said, "Seeing me each and every day aboard the battlestar, gents, causes you to take me for granted. My many admirable traits you overlook."

"I wish," said Apollo, "one of them was speed."

"It is." Starbuck climbed into his cockpit. "Didn't I only meet the young lady a matter of a few—"

"Are you still babbling about that awful hussy?" asked his computer.

"Howdy, Cora." Starbuck strapped himself into his seat. "Miss me?"

"Not a bit."

"Not even a little?"

"No, I made up my mind that if you're going to throw yourself at every pretty face that comes down the pike, well, I'm not going to sit here and fret."

"Ah, but I always come back to you, love." Starbuck grinned out at his two comrades. "I'll go aloft now, fellas. You stand by to execute your parts in our little surprise for the Cylons."

Apollo leaned close to him. "Remember, good buddy, that your ship isn't armed."

"That's not an item I'm likely to forget."

"Good luck," added Boomer.

"With my skill and Cora's brains, we don't need luck." He closed himself into the cockpit.

Apollo and Boomer moved clear of the Recon Viper One. In a moment, after a final grin and wave from Starbuck, the craft went roaring up from the surface of the planetoid.

"How many Cylons should we expect?" said Boomer, watching the Viper climb away.

"We'll soon find out," said Apollo.

Cora spotted them first.

"Oh, my," she said. "Here they come."

"Show me."

"Look at the display screen."

He noted three blips of greenish light on the dark screen. "Only three?"

"All armed to the teeth."

Exhaling smoke, Starbuck said, "Okay, pet, let's see if we can attract their attention."

"You absolutely certain you want to try this, hon?"

Starbuck grinned. "Be a shade late now if I was thinking of backing out." He punched out a course that would bring him close to the trio of approaching Cylon fighters.

"Going to be three against one," reminded the computer as they rushed toward the dangerous rendezvous.

"Three to three once Apollo and Boomer join in."

"But you don't have guns."

"But I'm armed with a superior brain," he said.

He could see the three formidable Cylon fighters growing ever larger outside his cockpit window.

"They'll fire in point-eight-five centons," the computer informed him.

"Okay, sweets, engage boosters a micron before they start shooting."

"Right you are, Bucky."

"And don't call me—"

The three Cylon ships had altered course and were heading right for Starbuck.

Their laserguns started to fire, etching lines of intense brightness across the black. But they didn't come near hitting him. The Viper had accelerated suddenly, swooping out of range.

"Hey, that was beautiful," exclaimed Starbuck as he banked the Viper.

"Yes, wasn't it," agreed Cora. "Oops! Here they come again. Hold on, hon."

The Cylons were diving, all three ships intent on catching up with Starbuck.

He executed a swift turn, accelerated again and once more eluded their banks of laserguns.

"What say we spring our trap now?" He banked and headed back for the planetoid. "I bet our Cylon buddies'll like this next little surprise."

CHAPTER TWENTY

"He's got 'em occupied," announced Apollo, checking his scanner screen. "Let's go, Boomer."

Instants later the captain's Viper blazed up from
the planetoid's surface. Boomer followed.

Both Vipers came up behind the trio of Cylon fighters that were intent on Starbuck. Apollo selected the
Cylon ship on the far right. He began shortening the
gap between them.

"Surprise," he said, firing his laserguns.

The shots flashed across the darkness separating
the ships.

The Cylon fighter glowed suddenly. It seemed to
hesitate for an instant, then exploded. The pieces rushed
away from each other.

The ship Boomer had gone after became aware of
him before he got in his first shot. It broke formation,
veering to the left. Boomer pursued. The third Cylon

fighter noticed him, too. Banking, it came diving at him.

"Whoops, that Cylon's after Boomer's tail," Starbuck said.

"Poor boy."

"Save the pity, Cora love," said the lieutenant. "Kick up the speed." He swung the Viper into an arc.

"Whatever are you planning?"

"I've got to make that Cylon idiot flinch and go off his course," explained Starbuck impatiently. "So we're going to have to cut in between him and Boomer. That'll—"

"That'll be like threading a needle."

"Kick us up to max speed."

"You can't take that. You'll black out."

"But you won't, kiddo. C'mon, let's move it."

Apollo witnessed the whole show, but he didn't quite believe it. He'd been swinging his Viper around to give Boomer a hand.

He saw that the second Cylon ship was closing in behind the lieutenant. He reached for his talkmike to give a warning.

But then something came whizzing across the darkness. It sizzled through the narrow gap between Boomer and his pursuer.

The Cylon swerved to avoid what he had to believe was a certain collision. Starbuck's ship got through the gap unscathed.

While that was happening, Boomer fired at the Cylon he was tailing. His second laser turned the Cylon fighter into jagged, scattering fragments.

Apollo sneaked up on the remaining Cylon ship, which was still a bit wobbly from its near encounter with Starbuck's very fast Recon Viper One.

Apollo fired his laserguns, and that took care of the last of the Cylon fighters.

"Boomer? You okay, buddy?"

"Yep, fine," answered the lieutenant. "Thanks, one and all, for the assistance."

"That was a handsome piece of flying, Starbuck." There was no answer.

"Starbuck?"

Cora said, "Oh, the poor boy's out cold."

"I told you it would hurt you. Now you're in a stupor, with your poor dear brains all scrambled and goodness knows what else is wrong—"

"Huh?"

"At least you can still mutter."

"Cora?" Starbuck blinked. "How'd we do?"

"Your little stunt worked."

He rubbed at his cheekbones. "So why are you so glum, my dear?"

"I thought you were dead or worse."

"Only a blackout," he assured her. "Is Boomer all right?"

"Yes. Captain Apollo destroyed the Cylon fighter that was after him," answered the computer. "Lieutenant Boomer took care of the other one."

"Hey, that's swell," said Starbuck. "Three out of three, that's a darn good score."

"I think you'd better allow me to run a full physical checkup on you," suggested Cora. "You can't tell what sort of dire and dreadful internal injuries you may have."

"I'm fine," he said. "Now let us return to Proteus."

"Must we?"

"Duty calls."

"Duty?" The computer produced a sniffing noise. "It's that awful outlaw woman."

CHAPTER TWENTY-ONE

Starbuck thumped himself on the chest. "I guarantee it," he said to Apollo. "I'm in crackerjack shape."

"You still look a bit glassy eyed, old buddy."

They were in the Proteus prison docking area, near their just-landed Vipers.

"He always looks that way," Boomer pointed out.

"I mean more so than usual." Apollo put a hand on Starbuck's shoulder. "A blackout like that can—"

"Really, granny, I'm fine." Starbuck took out a cigar. "I appreciate the concern, but I'm okay."

Boomer said, "That was a nice stunt you pulled, scaring that Cylon off my tail."

"With my new Viper, and my considerable skill, it's possible to do some pretty fancy flying," said Starbuck modestly.

"The Cylons may well send out more ships." Apollo was watching the freed prisoners who had scattered into small groups all around the overgrown spaceport.

"Meaning nobody's safe here on Proteus?" asked Boomer.

Starbuck lit his cigar. "Are we going to take 'em all back to the *Galactica?*" he asked. "If we use the shuttles and the enforcer ships we can mount a caravan that'll—"

"They may not all want to go," said Apollo.

"The charms of Proteus aren't that many," said Starbuck.

"Whatever's going to be done, it'll have to be done fast," said the captain. "We want to be back aboard the *Galactica* before any more Cylons show up in this galaxy."

"What you'd better do," Boomer suggested, "is gather one and all together and make a speech."

After the speech, which was short and to the point, Starbuck went searching for Robber.

He found her, sitting alone, at the edge of the field. Perching on a case beside her, he said, "Well?"

"Basically," the dark-haired young woman said, "I'm a solitary person."

"You sound like Scrapper."

Robber shrugged. "We're alike in some ways," she said. "I don't think I'm suited for refugee life with your fleet."

"You make it sound like you'll be all herded into pens or something," Starbuck said.

"I like the life I've established hereabouts. Moving around from asteroid to asteroid," she said. "Nobody criticizes me if I want to get off by myself once in a while, and I do like to do that."

He touched her hand. "But you tried to contact

Aeries," he reminded her. "You took my ship so you could travel there eventually."

"I was curious," Robber answered. "And restless. I get that way."

"Look," he said, "if I'm what's worrying you, forget it. I promise I won't shower you with attention once you're settled on the *Galactica*, won't act as though you're my best girl or—"

"No, I suppose you've got all sorts of other women who—"

"You're missing the point," he cut in. "I like you, Robber. Heck, I've proved that. What I'm saying is, once you get to the *Galactica* you won't be Starbuck's protégé. You can see as much or as little of me as you want."

"I understand, yes."

"I don't know if you do or not, when you use that sad, little girl tone on me," he said. "What I'm really anxious about is that you get the hell off Proteus. There's a very strong possibility that more Cylons'll be coming this way before long."

She said, "I heard the prisoners talking while you were away. Many of them want to stay right here."

"Here? On Proteus? Why would—"

"It's home to them. They believe they can grow enough crops to survive."

"The Cylons may not let 'em survive."

"Everything in life's a gamble."

"Granted some people would prefer to be farmers and not relocate to the fleet," he conceded. "That doesn't apply to you."

"That's true, but—"

"Hold it," he said, holding up his hand. "How about a compromise? Some of the ex-prisoners will want to come with us. We're going to need good pilots to fly the shuttles and fighter ships. You're an excellent flyer."

"There are others, just as good."

"But not as attractive. Why don't you at least fly a load of passengers to the battlestar," he suggested. "Take a look around, see if you like things there. If you don't, you can always come back here."

Robber considered his suggestion. "Well, I do owe you a favor," she said, "since I caused you quite a bit of trouble."

"You don't *owe* me a darn thing, but if you want—"

"I'll do it," she said.

"Great." He hugged her.

"They're committing suicide," said Boomer.

"We can't force anyone to come with us," Apollo said.

"Look on the bright side," put in Starbuck. "We may be able to take care of whatever Cylons stick their noses into this part of the universe."

"Tangling with Cylons isn't my idea of a good time," said the lieutenant.

"And we have no way of knowing how many ships they'll send next time." Apollo moved closer to his Viper.

About two dozen of the freed Proteus prisoners wanted to come along back to the *Galactica*. Roughly twice that number had voted to remain.

Three commandeered shuttles were loaded with passengers and, at Starbuck's suggestion, crates of the surplus Ambrosa. Robber, who was going to be piloting the lead shuttle, was supervising its loading.

Starbuck, puffing on his cigar, watched her while he and his fellow warriors talked.

"The folks who're staying," said Boomer, "deserve a chance to make a go of it. If the Cylons come—"

"Starbuck may be right," said Apollo. "We can try to stop that from happening."

"For a while maybe," said Boomer. "But we can only knock out so many of their fighters."

"Why so sad lookin'?" Scrapper, grinning, had come over to them.

Starbuck said, "Boomer always puddles up at farewells and leavetakings."

"Way I see it, there's a plan for everythin'," said Scrapper. "Folks get together and they separate and it all works out in the end. Most times anyhow."

Starbuck asked him, "You sure you don't want to tag along?"

"Yep, but thanks for repeatin' the invite," he said. "I just wasn't meant for livin' with a whole mess of folks, Starbuck."

"You'd fit right in on the battlestar," Starbuck told him. "With that trick arm of yours, you could do all sorts of handy—"

"Nope, I aim to stay around here." He pointed skyward with his metal thumb. "Here and over to the planetoid where we first met up."

Giving a resigned shrug, Starbuck said, "Okay. Wish you'd come, though."

Scrapper leaned closer to him. "Do me one favor, though," he said quietly. "Take care of Robber, see she does okay."

"I will," promised Starbuck.

CHAPTER TWENTY-TWO

Upon his pedestal the Imperious Leader said, "You do not bring me good news?"

The Centurion acknowledged that with a slight bow. "May I speak?"

"Do so."

"The three fighter ships that were sent to investigate the signals being sent to Aeries have ceased to communicate. I conclude they have been destroyed."

The pedestal flashed and flickered in the dim room. The Cylon leader ordered, "Three more ships must be sent."

"It will be done at once."

"They are to make a full report."

Bowing deeply, the Centurion left the room.

When Commander Adama stepped onto the bridge of the *Galactica,* Colonel Tigh, looking pleased, came striding over to him.

"The news is good," said Tigh.

"So I hear."

"Apollo and Boomer have found Starbuck," continued the colonel. "He and Recon Viper One are in good shape."

Adama nodded.

"They encountered three ships," Tigh said. "All three were destroyed."

"We seem to have won," Adama said, "for the moment."

"Since the Cylons are gone, we won't have to change course," Tigh said. "That means the Vipers and the other ships will be able to rendezvous with us."

"Other ships?"

"They're leading a convoy of several shuttles," explained Colonel Tigh. "Bringing people who've been rescued from an asteroid called Proteus."

"We can accommodate them, I'm sure."

"According to Apollo, most of our visitors have been residing in a prison on Proteus."

"They're criminals?"

Tigh said, "Apollo assures me they're not. He'll explain everything when they arrive, with some help from Lieutenant Starbuck."

"Yes, I imagine Starbuck will have quite a report to make." Adama glanced toward a window and the blackness outside.

"I've alerted the docking area."

Commander Adama said, "The Cylons don't like being beaten."

"Few warriors do."

"They'll almost certainly send more ships out here."

"We're ready for them."

"I hope so," said the commander.

• • •

Athena sat alone at a table in the lounge. Her slim back was turned to the view windows and she seemed to be concentrating on the forefinger she was tapping against the side of her glass.

"Mind if I join you?"

"I guess not...oh, it's you."

Cassiopea took the chair opposite. "Feeling down-hearted?"

"Especially so now that you're here, Cass dear."

The blonde smiled tentatively. "I dropped over to suggest a truce," she said.

Looking up, Athena said, "We're not at war."

"I know, but—"

"In order to have a war the two opposing parties have to be contesting the ownership of some valuable piece of property."

Cassiopea said, "And you're implying that Star-buck isn't valuable enough to feud over?"

"Right," replied Athena. "On top of which, I'm not at all interested in owning him—even for a short spell of time."

"He is sort of a rat, isn't he? Attempting to take us both to dinner, pretending that each of us was—"

"Starbuck wouldn't have tried that, dear, unless you'd forced yourself on him and insisted—"

"Me?" Cassiopea touched her breast. "It was you, sweet, who horned in on—"

"Is this your notion of truce talks?"

"You're right." Cassiopea relaxed in her chair. "I think you've adopted the right attitude. He's not worth arguing about."

"Especially now."

She sat up. "What's so special about now?" she asked, frowning. "He's safely on his way home, isn't he?"

"Oh, sure. But he's bringing several shuttles full of young women with him."

"He is? How'd he manage that?"

"They're escaped convicts or something," explained Athena. "He rescued them off an asteroid. The details in Apollo's message were sketchy."

"Well, then you don't know if it's Starbuck who's responsible for bringing them back or Apollo or Boomer."

Athena tilted her head, eyeing the other young woman. "Do you really doubt that it's Starbuck who came up with the idea?"

"I guess not."

"Exactly."

CHAPTER TWENTY-THREE

Cora the computer said, "It's a real shame."

"What is?" inquired Starbuck.

"The way you're carrying on," she told him.

"I was under the impression I was carrying on admirably."

"As an example," said Cora, "let me mention the manner in which you're behaving at this very moment."

"Ah, I get your drift, kiddo."

He had cut the speed of his Recon Viper One and dropped back to see how the shuttle that Robber was piloting was faring.

"Here you have a ship," said the computer, "that can just zip along through space and you're dawdling back here like—"

"We're *escorting* these ships back to the battlestar," he reminded her. "That means we keep an eye on them. This isn't a race."

"From what I've seen of that hussy, she can more than take care of herself."

"You're letting Robber's front fool you," the lieutenant said. "Inside she's not anywhere near as—"

"And, my, isn't that a lovely name? Won't that sound just marvelous after you're married? 'How do you do. My name's Robber Starbuck and—'"

"Whoa there, Cora," he interrupted. "I don't intend to get hitched to Robber or anyone else. Simply because I take an interest in a young lady doesn't mean—"

"Oh, I know all about the kind of interest you take in young women. I've scanned your dossier, from the time you—"

"If you have, then you know what a nice cleancut fellow I am." He took out a cigar, lit it. "Women think of me as a protector of their best interests."

"Hogwash."

"They sure built some strange stuff into you," observed Starbuck. "I'm starting to think you're jealous."

"Oh, my," exclaimed the computer.

"What?"

"I'm getting something on my scanners," Cora replied.

"Cylons?"

"Afraid so, hon," she answered ruefully. "Three more of them, coming right this way."

Robber had been trying to concentrate on piloting the shuttle, not wanting to think about what things would be like aboard the battlestar *Galactica*. She was aware of Starbuck's Viper out there keeping an eye on her.

She was really going to have to sort out her—

"...don't you?"

Robber realized that Assault, who was sitting in the seat beside her, had asked her a question. "What's that?"

"I was saying we're doing the right thing," the bearded man repeated.

"Yes, I agree."

"But I get the feeling that you haven't made up your mind."

"I think I have, though."

"How long have you known him?"

"Starbuck? Not long, not very long at all."

Assault scratched at his beard. "I didn't think so, but I got the impression you were pretty close."

"That happens sometimes. You meet somebody, you feel as though you've been friends all along."

"Hard for me to judge," he said. "In the prison...well, you know how that was. You grow up with the same people, the same enforcers even. There wasn't much chance to meet anyone new."

"You'll sure have a chance to meet new people on the *Galactica*," Robber told him. "All sorts of people."

Nodding, Assault said, "You've always had more nerve than most of us. Leaving prison when you were just a kid, going out on your own—"

"I wasn't exactly a kid, I was seventeen," Robber said. "After my mother died, I knew I had to get out and away."

"You figure you'll stay on the *Galactica*?"

"For a while," she answered. "Until I get restless."

He stared out the window for a moment. "And you're not scared at all?"

Robber said, "A little uneasy maybe. I'm not exactly what you'd call ladylike and I don't want to be taken for some kind of rustic bumpkin."

Assault chuckled. "You don't have to worry about that," he assured her.

"We'll see."

"I understand what's bothering you. You figure that when Starbuck gets a look at you alongside the ladies of the *Galactica*, he'll decide you're not sophisticated enough."

"Something like that."

Assault scratched his whiskers again. "Of course, I haven't seen any of those ladies myself," he said. "But I think you'll measure up okay."

"Thanks," she said.

"It's going to be different, living on a gigantic spacecraft that's always on the move."

"Won't be as cramped as prison," she said. "And eventually, according to what Captain Apollo said, the *Galactica* will reach its destination."

"Earth," murmured Assault. "Could be there isn't any such place."

"I believe there is."

"Why?"

Robber said, "Mostly because *they* believe in it so intensely. Apollo, Boomer and Starbuck."

"Hold on to your hats, kids," came Starbuck's voice out of the talkbox on the control panel. "Or better yet, man your defense guns."

"What is it?" asked Robber.

"Reliable sources, namely my trusty computer Cora, inform me that there are more Cylons on the way," said Starbuck.

"That sounds bad," said Robber.

"Things could be worse."

"How?"

After a moment he answered, "Well, actually I can't think of any examples right now. So get your guns ready, keep a weather eye out and cross your fingers. Looks like we got another battle coming up."

Starbuck asked, "You see 'em yet, Apollo, old buddy?"

"Yep, here they come now," answered the captain. "Three ships."

"That's not so bad. They could've sent half a dozen this time around."

"That could be what they'll try next."

"I'm going to hang back here and watch out for the shuttles," said Starbuck into his talkmike.

"Those crates are armed," said Apollo, "but I don't think they're any match for Cylon fighters."

"We'll have to make do with what we got."

"Talk to you soon, chum. Got to greet our visitors."

Starbuck took a puff of his cigar and squinted out his cockpit window.

Far ahead in the darkness of space he could just make out the two Vipers going into action against the oncoming Cylon ships.

He picked up his talkmike once more, and contacted Robber. "I've got visual contact with our friends now," he told her. "Three fighters, like the ones we tangled with earlier."

"Do you think Apollo and Boomer can hold them off?"

"I'll bet on it, but... hey, wow! Apollo got one of 'em!"

The exploding Cylon fighter made an enormous

splash of red and yellow across the blackness.

"Be nice if they can take out the other two," came Robber's voice. "Because when we checked our laserguns, Starbuck, we discovered only one is functioning."

"What? Didn't anybody think to look the guns over before we left?"

"We took our leave, if you recall, in something of a hurry."

"Yeah, I remember."

"We've got Forger tinkering with the guns," she told him. "He's handy with gadgets."

"Let's hope he's also fast."

"I can dodge pretty well," Robber said. "So maybe—"

"Hold on! A Cylon's gotten past Boomer. He's coming our way."

"At you?"

"I think," said Starbuck, "he's got you in mind, kid."

"Damn," remarked Lieutenant Boomer.

He executed a loop to get on the tail of the Cylon fighter that had managed to outfox him. The Cylon was racing toward the first shuttle ship.

"She's a tough lady," said Boomer, "but I don't think she can outfly that Cylon. Not in a clunky crate like that."

He increased his speed, narrowing the distance between him and the fighter. Then Boomer became aware of Starbuck.

Starbuck was diving straight at the Cylon. He was racing across space at nearly max speed. There was no way he could avoid colliding with the Cylon.

"Starbuck," yelled Boomer into his talkmike, "pull up, you idiot! You'll smash!"

Starbuck was hunched in the pilot seat of Recon Viper One, cigar clenched in his teeth. "Don't let me down, Cora my love."

"One of these days," she chided, "your daredevil ways are going to be the ruin of—"

"Got a hunch today ain't the day, love."

"The odds in favor of our smashing right into this vile Cylon craft and—"

"In my wild youth we used to play a similar game in skycars," he informed the computer as they rushed down toward the fighter that was stalking Robber. "We called the game Chicken."

"A childish male—"

"Stand by, Cora."

If the Cylon didn't flinch and dodge out of Starbuck's path, there was going to be an impressive collision.

"That damn fool," said Assault. "He's done for."

"Starbuck knows what he's doing," insisted Robber as she strived to maneuver the rattletrap shuttle away from the pursuing Cylon fighter.

"What he's doing is committing suicide," said the bearded man.

The Cylon gave in at the last instant, pulling up and flashing away from the shuttle.

Starbuck's Viper whizzed across the path of the slow-moving shuttle.

Lieutenant Boomer's Viper came roaring over.

Before the Cylon could complete its turn, Boomer's guns sliced across the blackness.

The needles of light dug into the belly of the Cylon

fighter. The ship began vibrating, shivering and shuddering. Then it blew up.

Robber sighed. "He saved us," she said.

"Everybody intact aboard?" inquired Starbuck.

"We are. And you?"

"Fit as a fiddle," he answered.

"I didn't realize how suicidal you were, but thanks."

"Don't start sounding like my beloved Cora," Starbuck warned. "It ain't suicide when you know exactly what you're doing. And in case our late Cylon chum hadn't buzzed off, I still could've swerved and tried another trick or two."

"I appreciate your interest," she said.

"You may not have noticed," added Starbuck, "but Apollo took care of the remaining Cylon while Boomer and I were playing games here. Therefore, kiddo, we ought to have a safe and sound journey home."

CHAPTER TWENTY-FOUR

Starbuck said, "Cora, I want to thank you for a most interesting jaunt." He unfastened his safety gear.

"I guess this is goodbye," said the computer in a downcast voice.

"Hey, we'll be flying together again." Starbuck glanced out at the *Galactica* docking area. A crew moved toward his just-landed ship.

"I . . . I'll miss you."

"Same here, love." Opening the cockpit, he stepped out.

Cora made a sad, sighing sound.

Starbuck stretched, scratched, dug out a fresh cigar.

"I'm amazed," said Apollo, walking to Starbuck's side.

"By what? The sheer artistry of my flying?"

"Your incredible luck."

133

"You call it luck, but actually it's skill. Pure skill." They moved over to the area where the shuttles would be docking.

"Well, I have to admit you handled that new Viper damn well."

"I did," agreed Starbuck, pausing to light a new cigar.

"Think she'll fit in?"

The first shuttle was coming in now.

"Robber? Sure, she's adaptable."

"The young lady is fond of you."

"Most all females..." Starbuck frowned and turned serious for a moment. "I know. I feel responsible for her and...I like her, too."

"But?"

"I'm just not ready to limit myself to any one woman."

"I think she knows that, old buddy."

Starbuck nodded. "Well, let's go over and play reception committee," he suggested.

Athena said, "Which one do you think it is?"

Cassiopea said, "Why limit ourselves to one? It could be a whole bunch."

The two young women were standing at the edge of the group that was watching the shuttles dock and unload their passengers.

"That blonde there?" suggested Athena.

"Nope." Cassiopea gave a negative shake of her head. "She's too...um...ample."

"Don't forget that Starbuck likes obvious blondes."

"Not that obvious, dear."

"How about the redhead?"

"Too skinny," decided Cassiopea. "Starbuck does

sometimes show an interest in underweight women, as you know, but—"

"There he is, pushing his way up to the disembark doors of that shuttle."

"Yes, and he's getting rid of his cigar."

"That means," concluded Athena, "that he's getting ready to greet someone special."

"That big man with the beard? That can't be right."

"Well, they are shaking hands—very cordially."

"I know Starbuck. He didn't nudge his way up there just to pass out a hearty handshake."

"You're right. Look at him now," said Athena, disapproval in her voice.

"He's giving a real bearhug to that filthy girl."

"She's a child, not more than twenty."

"Taller than he is, too."

"Well, he's always saying he wants a woman he can look up to."

"Look at the way she's returning his embrace," pointed out Cassiopea. "She's obviously fond of him."

"Do you think that what she's wearing is considered fashionable in this galaxy?"

"I hope not. Those trousers of hers are only a few steps from being rags."

"I don't think much of her hair," observed Athena. "Too long, too unkempt."

"Color's dreadful, too. Sort of a dull, sooty black."

"It may not really be that dark. She obviously doesn't wash very often." Athena sighed, shaking her head. "Do you think the new Viper has possibly affected his brain?"

"He was already showing lapses in taste before he took off," said Cassiopea. "When he took you to dinner I knew something was going on wrong."

"I'm not talking about his lapses in taste before he left," said Athena. "Even though his being seen with you indicates some kind of extreme mental—"

"Look, we better not squabble. What's obviously called for is a united front."

Athena nodded. "Yes, you're absolutely right, Cass," she agreed. "We must unite against a common enemy."

"Once we've taken care of her, then we can get back to our own . . . oops! Watch out, Starbuck seems to be bringing her right over here to us."

"Ladies," said Starbuck, grinning as he guided Robber up to the two of them. "I want you both to meet a good friend of mine. I'm sure you're all going to become fast friends."

"Oh, of course," smiled Athena.

"Oh, certainly," smiled Cassiopea.

Robber was sitting on the edge of the bunk, legs dangling. Her left eye was slightly narrowed and she was taking in the cabin she'd been assigned to. "Homier than a prison cell," she decided, "if not a hell of a lot bigger."

Standing, she explored the room. She opened a door and observed, "Nice plumbing facilities, too."

Pausing, she studied her image in the mirror on the inside of the door.

She was going to have to shape up some. She did look a little wild and unkempt, compared to the women she'd seen so far on the *Galactica*.

"First thing to do is wash up, then try on these new clothes they—"

Someone was tapping on the door of her quarters.

"Come on in," she invited.

"You have to activate the door, kiddo."

"Yeah, that's right." She scooted over to flip the right switch. "Now come in."

Starbuck, decked out in a fresh warrior uniform, stood on the threshold. He clutched a bunch of crimson flowers in his right hand; in his left was a smoldering cigar. "For you, my love," he said, handing in the bouquet and then coming into the room himself.

"They're pretty," she said as she took the flowers.

"Finest plastic blooms to be found aboard the entire battlestar," he assured her.

Smiling, Robber placed them on a small table. "Flowers always brighten up a room," she said. "Sit someplace, why don't you?"

"Thanks, I will." He settled into one of the cabin's two chairs. "Like the joint?"

"More or less."

"Going to take some getting used to."

"You remember our agreement." She sat again on the edge of the bunk. "I'm only trying this out. I can take off anytime."

"Sure, the *Galactica* isn't a prison."

"I know, the plumbing's too good for that," she said. "So just make sure nobody junks that shuttle I flew in on. I may want to use it again some day."

He grinned. "This evening, or what passes for evening hereabouts, we're going to have a sort of celebration in the rec lounge," he informed her. "To welcome all you pilgrims aboard. Music, dancing, libations and fun for the whole family."

Robber shrugged. "Do you really want me to go?"

"Why not?"

She answered, "Those two girls you introduced me to. Athena and Cassiopea....I didn't miss the way they were inspecting me from tip to toe."

"Envy, my child, pure and simple."

"No, they're both fond of you." She brushed at her long dark hair. "They were obviously wondering why the hell you were showing an interest in in some wild savage from the sticks."

"Hey, I've seen a few savages in my days," Starbuck said. "You aren't one, Robber."

"There's another problem," the young woman said. "When you told them my name, one of them could hardly keep from snickering and the other one just looked stunned."

"C'mon, kid. Being named Cassiopea isn't all that nifty either," he pointed out.

"But I ought to have a real name," she told him with conviction. "My mother never knew our family name. That's one of the reasons I was anxious to reach Aeries, to find out who I really am."

"You're not going to be able to do that, not with the Cylons in control of the planet," he said. "Tell you what.... Why don't we just pick a new name for you? One you can use until you find out the true and authentic one."

"I suppose I could do that," Robber said. "Any suggestions?"

"How about Roberta? It's close to the name you're using now."

"Roberta sounds like a prissy blonde," she said, "with freckles."

"Merely a suggestion."

"Do you like the sound of Roberta?"

"Sure," he said. "It has a certain lilt."

"I'll think about it," she said finally. "But I'm not promising anything."

"Feel free to pick one of your own." Starbuck stood up. "Got to take my leave. But if you don't mind, I'll drop by this eve to escort you to the festivities."

"You don't have to."

"I know I don't have to," he said. "I want to."

"Okay then, it's a date." Crossing the room, she gave him a quick but careful kiss on the cheek. "Thanks again. For everything."

Apollo paced his father's quarters as he spoke. "So that's the story of Proteus and its prison," he concluded.

"Incredible," said Colonel Tigh, who sat in a chair across from Adama. "Going on like that, generation after generation, cut off from everything."

"In a way," observed the commander, who sat with his chin resting on steepled fingers, "their situation parallels ours."

"But we have a mission and a purpose," said Tigh.

"They thought they did, too," said Adama.

"You're not suggesting we're as deluded as they are?"

"No." Commander Adama smiled. "Only that I noted some similarities. At any rate, we shall do everything in our power to make them welcome on the *Galactica*."

Apollo sat down. "There's also the problem of those who chose to stay behind on Proteus."

"Yes. If the Cylons learn of them," said the Colonel, "they're doomed."

Adama asked his son, "Do they have anything in the way of defenses?"

"Some antiquated fighter ships, a few shuttles similar to the ones you saw earlier. The ships are armed with laser weapons, but not one is a match for a Cylon fighter."

"We better make sure the Cylons decide this particular galaxy isn't worth the trouble."

"Lessons like that," pointed out the colonel, "are hard to teach."

"We'll find a way."

Apollo asked, "You're expecting them to send more fighters out here, aren't you?"

"I am, yes."

Tigh leaned forward in his chair. "I anticipate a new Cylon attack, too," he said. "In light of that, do you think it's wise to hold the welcoming party this evening?"

Commander Adama said, "Yes, since it will make our new guests feel at home and it will be good for the morale of our people."

"If there's an attack, we—"

"We'll be ready," Adama assured him.

CHAPTER TWENTY-FIVE

Starbuck took his cigar from between his lips. "Wow," he remarked.

Smiling tentatively, Robber asked him, "Do I look okay?"

He nodded affirmatively, moving into her room from the corridor. "You did something to your hair."

"Washed it, cut it a bit."

"And you're using makeup."

"Just a little. You don't think it's too much?"

"Nope, it's just right." He held his cigar at arm's length before sniffing the air. "Perfume, too?"

"Supposed to smell like wild flowers," she said. "Although I've never sniffed any wild flowers that smelled this musky. Not too strong, is it?"

"It's very delicate, don't worry."

Taking a step back from him, she held her arms out at her side. "Now how about the clothes, Starbuck? Just standard issue, but do they look okay and fit right?"

"Yep," he assured her, "yep, they fit. Just fine."

"Why are you looking at me in that dippy, sort of cockeyed way?"

The lieutenant shook his head. "You're really . . . pretty."

"Hadn't you noticed that up till now?"

"I noticed, sure . . . but you didn't look like this out on the asteroids and planetoids, kid."

"Well, that's because I was wearing my work clothes," she explained. "But, hell, once I got a look at the competition around here, I realized I better upgrade my image."

"You've succeeded. Darn well."

"I don't want you to feel responsible for me in any way," Robber said. "But still there are people aboard this battlestar . . . Athena and Cass to name just two . . . who are going to think of me as your protégé. For a while, anyhow. So I want to make damn sure you're not embarrassed by me."

"Those feelings you can lay to rest, Robber."

"And I've decided I will be Roberta," she said. "For now at least."

Grinning, he offered her his arm. "Roberta," he invited, "allow me to escort you to the celebration."

Lieutenant Jolly was among the first to notice her. Smoothing his moustache, he came ambling across the crowded rec lounge to Starbuck. "Well, great to see you back safe and sound, Starbuck," Jolly said, his eyes on Robber and his hand extended to the lieutenant.

Starbuck shook hands. "Like you to meet a friend

of mine. Robb...Roberta, this is the one and only Lieutenant Jolly. Jolly, Roberta."

Jolly, much to Starbuck's surprise, clicked his booted heels, bowed, took Robber's right hand and planted a kiss on it. "Charmed," he said.

"So am I, Lieutenant," she said, smiling. "I've heard a great deal about you since I arrived."

"You have?"

Starbuck said, "Mostly dire warnings, I imagine."

"Some of the girls dropped in to say hello," explained Robber. "Naturally, they got around to mentioning their favorite men aboard the *Galactica*."

Chuckling, Lieutenant Jolly asked, "And I was one of 'em, huh?"

"Your name just about headed the list."

"Fancy that," said Jolly, chuckling further.

"It is hard to believe, isn't it?" Starbuck glanced around the lounge.

He was less than pleased to notice that several other young warriors had detached themselves from their groups to come heading this way.

"If we should get separated, Roberta," he said, "you have but to let out a yell and I'll come to the rescue."

Jolly told her, "Why, you're in no danger here."

Four more lieutenants converged on them.

Apollo found Starbuck staring out a window of the lounge. "You seem far from festive, good buddy."

"True."

"Must I remind you that this is a party? The purpose of parties is to cheer people up."

Starbuck took a slow sip from his glass of Ambrosa. "All through history it has been ever thus."

"What has?"

"Need you ask?" Turning away from the window, he gestured at the large cluster of young men across the room. "Know who's at the heart of that huddle?"

"Robber."

"Correct." Starbuck stared into his drink for a silent moment. "All through history the great discoverers, inventors, explorers and men of courage have gone forth and brought back great treasures and then ended up with the short end of the stick."

"I've heard that before, though not exactly in those words."

"I found Robb . . . Roberta. That's her new name, by the way. Another of my inventions, I might add. I discovered Roberta on a remote asteroid and brought her hence."

"I thought she found you and conked you on the head."

"The point is, if you'll cease heckling and heaping scorn on me in my hour of need," continued Starbuck sadly, "the point is, I discovered this lady, persuaded her to come here and . . . I'm ignored. Cast aside while flocks of randy youths surround her."

"So, why not give her a chance to meet people?"

"Am I standing in her way? Heck, if I did I'd only end up getting trampled."

"Jealous, maybe?"

Starbuck considered. "Well, I did expect to spend some time with her at this shindig," he admitted. "She looks absolutely terrific tonight, doesn't she?"

"I noticed." Apollo smiled. "Suppose you devote some time to Cass or Athena and—"

"They're having nothing to do with me."

"Neither one?"

"Both gave me what you might call the cold shoulder." He drank a little more of his drink.

"Looking at things from a more rational point of view," said Apollo, "you ought to be pleased. Earlier you were concerned that Robber might not fit in here on the *Galactica*. It sure looks like she's a social success."

"She doesn't have to be *that* successful," complained Starbuck.

"This'll settle down eventually. Then you can—"

"Attention!" boomed the overhead speakers. "All personnel report to battle stations at once! Repeat! All—"

"Looks like we've got something else to worry about," said Apollo.

CHAPTER TWENTY-SIX

Alarm sirens were sounding. Protective shields were dropping into place over the windows of the rec lounge.

Starbuck hurried toward the exit. Robber caught him by the arm. "What is it, what's wrong?"

"My guess'd be a Cylon raid."

She lowered her head. "I was afraid of that," she said. "It's my fault for being stupid enough to try to contact—"

"Hey, we've been having trouble with the Cylons for quite a spell now," he said. "Long before you came along."

"Yes, but you know what I mean. I—"

"We'll have a nice long talk soon as I get back from the wars," he promised.

She tightened her grip on his arm. "Can I do something? Fly a—"

"Stick here and keep all our new arrivals from

panicking," he suggested. "A Cylon raid on their first day here can't make 'em feel any too chipper."

"Okay." She kissed him on the cheek. "Come back."

"Such is my intention." He left her, left the big room.

Lieutenant Jolly fell in beside him and they moved along a corridor together. "What's the story?"

"Cylons are probably attacking us and—"

"No, I mean with you and Roberta," said the moustached lieutenant impatiently. "I noticed that leave-taking just now. She likes you."

"Sure, that's why she spent the evening allowing oafs like you to hover all—"

"Aw, it's not who they chitchat with at the party that's important," Jolly told him, "it's who they go home with. Or is that whom?"

"It's hooey either way."

"If I get back from this mission," said Jolly, "I intend to try to cut you off. Just thought I'd be fair and warn—"

"*If* you get back?" Starbuck shook his head. "Quit talking like that, Jolly, or you'll jinx us all."

Commander Adama entered the *Galactica* bridge. "What's the latest?"

The wail of warning alarms and the slamming of metal doors echoed all around.

When the commander reached a scanner screen, Colonel Tigh said, "It appears to be a full-scale attack."

Adama, brows knit, watched the blips of light moving ominously across the screen. "Fifty Cylon fighters," he observed.

"And they're coming right for us," said Tigh. "Not

heading for Proteus or any of the other asteroids out there."

"They may not know there's any human life on the asteroids," the commander said. "If we stop them, it's possible they'll never find out."

"The Cylons certainly know *we're* here."

"That was, quite probably, inevitable."

"The young woman who tried to contact Aeries," said the colonel as he watched the screen. "I understand she's now aboard the battlestar."

"Yes, I met her when our new guests arrived," answered Adama. "Is the Blue Squadron ready to launch?"

"A few microns yet," said Tigh. "Many of the warrior pilots were at the party, so it's taking them longer to—"

"I'm still glad we had the celebration."

"I wasn't implying any criticism, Commander, simply stating facts."

Adama nodded. "The young lady, Robber she's called, piloted one of the shuttles," he said. "I don't believe she deliberately tried to contact the Cylons."

"You're taking her on face value?"

"No," said the commander. "Both Starbuck and my son vouch for her. And that counts for something."

"Didn't this same young woman try to murder Starbuck?"

"Not according to the lieutenant's report," said Adama. "There was simply a misunderstanding during which Lieutenant Starbuck happened to get hit, quite accidentally, on the head."

"I haven't met the young woman," said Colonel Tigh. "I'm assuming, however, that she's attractive."

"Very much so," said Adama. "But I've never

found, Colonel, that a pretty woman is any less trustworthy than a plain one."

"I don't imagine Lieutenant Starbuck has either."

From a voicebox came, "Blue Squadron ready to launch!"

"Good luck," murmured the commander.

Starbuck shot a quick glance over to where Recon Viper One was sitting, then climbed into his regular Viper. "Going to miss you, Cora," he said. "But I'm going to need my guns this time out."

He strapped himself in, shut the cockpit and began checking out his instruments.

"Going to miss that extra speed, too."

Lieutenant Boomer's voice came out of a grid on the dash. "How you doing, Starbuck?"

"Raring to go."

"You looked mighty gloomy at the party."

"Me? You're mistaken, chum," Starbuck assured him. "On several occasions, in fact, folks in my vicinity had to warn me to hush up because I was laughing and carrying on with such vigor."

"Your lady friend was, beyond a doubt, the hit of the evening."

Starbuck didn't reply.

"Starbuck?"

"He just stepped out onto the terrace," said Starbuck. "Any message?"

"Geeze, you sound awful grumpy for a guy who's supposed to be bubbling over with happiness."

"Hey, what are you, Boomer? Some Cylon agent sent to demoralize me or what?"

"Seemed obvious to me that Robber favors you above all others," Boomer told him. "In case that's what you're moping about. Just because Jolly and a bunch of the other guys were flocking around her like—"

"Roberta," corrected Starbuck. "She's decided to call herself Roberta from hence onward. It sounds a bit less larcenous than Robber."

"Ready to launch," announced a metallic voice.

"We'll continue this conversation," promised Boomer, "when we return."

"No hurry," said Starbuck.

CHAPTER TWENTY-SEVEN

Captain Apollo fired his lasers again. He scored another direct hit on one of the oncoming Cylon fighters. The enemy ship burst, sending glittering fragments spewing in all directions across the darkness.

"Hey," came Starbuck's puzzled voice, "what the heck is going on here?"

Apollo answered, "Not sure, old buddy."

"These bozos aren't fighting back at all," said Starbuck. "What're they up to?"

"You've got me. But we might as well take advantage of it."

"Well, sure. But it ain't exactly sporting." Starbuck signed off.

Two Cylons were coming right for Apollo's Viper. He dived, banked and came up beneath them. His laserguns fired into the underside of one of the Cylon fighters. The craft turned into a scattering, spinning mess of debris.

"Now where the heck did the other one get to?"

Banking again, he spotted the Cylon.

The ship had broken through the Vipers that ringed the *Galactica*.

It was hurtling straight for the battlestar.

"Attention, *Galactica!*" Apollo said into his talk-mike. "One of 'em's through and heading right for you."

"Our laser turrets can handle him," said Adama's voice.

Apollo was watching the hurtling Cylon fighter. "Dad, he's not going to fire on you," he warned. "He's going to ram!"

A micron later the Cylon hit the *Galactica*, its snout ripping into the side of the battlestar.

"That's what they're up to," realized Apollo. "It's a suicide mission. They're trying to destroy the *Galactica!*"

Robber had been sitting at a small table in the now quiet rec lounge. Her arm rested on the slick tabletop, close to her untouched glass of Ambrosa.

Across from her, nervously drumming his stubby fingers on the table, sat Assault. "Quite a welcome," he remarked.

The sounds of the space battle outside could be heard dimly in the lounge.

"It's called reality," the young woman said, smiling faintly. "Might as well learn to deal with it right off."

"I know," said the bearded man. "Trouble is, I really would hate to get killed my first day aboard."

"As I understand it," she said, "this battlestar is built to withstand quite a lot. They've been through plenty of attacks and survived every damn one."

"So far." Assault glanced around the room.

The former prisoners were seated at various tables, hunched and silent for the most part.

"Think of it this way," Robber said. "You're better off here than you were on Proteus."

"Sure, but on Proteus I didn't have to worry about Cylons."

"That didn't mean they couldn't have attacked at any time and wiped out everybody on the asteroid."

"Sure, but I didn't know about that possibility." Assault scratched at his beard. "Even so, the—"

"And you don't have Croad to annoy you anymore."

"Funny about him," said Assault. "Deciding to stay on Proteus and throw in with the others."

"The guy's stubborn as hell," she said. "A trait like that ought to come in handy for a farmer."

"I keep wondering if—"

There was an enormous boom, then the sound of metal being torn, ripped and twisted.

The floor of the lounge shook and bounced. The tables rattled and swayed. All the lights in the big room died.

A moment later someone said in the thick darkness, "I don't hear the aircirc system anymore. We're not getting any air!"

Commander Adama turned toward the colonel. "How bad so far?"

"Two Cylon fighters have broken through," answered Tigh. "Both hit us starboard. The damage is being assessed now."

"It's probably not major."

Athena was at her console. "The power is down in that area," she said.

The commander asked her, "Does that include the rec lounge?"

"Afraid so."

"What about the aux system?"

Athena shook her head. "That's not functioning either."

Adama locked his hands behind his back, watching his daughter's screen. "Then there's no light or air?"

"That's right."

"How many people still in the room?"

"All our new arrivals, or just about," answered Athena. "It was assumed they'd be safe in the rec lounge."

"None of the exit doors are functioning?"

"No, which means everyone is trapped inside."

Adama asked Tigh, "How soon can we get the power supply repaired, Colonel?"

Shaking his head, Tigh answered, "Not until the attack is over, Commander."

"Can we get a crew to the lounge, to let those people out?"

"We can try," the colonel said. "But we don't know how many frozen and jammed doors they'll have to get through to reach there."

"Send a crew, instruct them to look for anyone trapped in that entire area," ordered Commander Adama. "How long can the people in the rec lounge survive on what air is there?"

"It's possible there's enough air to last until we can reach them," said Tigh. "But there are quite a few people there."

Adama said, "Very well. Do what you can, Colonel."

"Let's everybody calm down," Robber said in a commanding voice.

"We're all going to die," wailed someone in the darkness.

"You sure as hell will if you don't shut up," she warned him. "I'll see to it myself. Where are those damn lights?"

"Coming up, miss." Over beside the bar two hand-lights blossomed.

Robber said, "Bring me one, then see if you can find any more."

"Right you are," answered the bartender, trotting through the huddled figures to her side.

Robber took the light, then swept its small beam around the big room. "Forger? Where the hell are you?"

"Haven't seen him," volunteered Adulteress.

"He was here," said Robber with certainty. "Forger! Get your ancient butt in gear."

"I'm dying, child," croaked a feeble voice.

Robber pointed with the beam of light. "There he is, ducked under that table. Assault, drag him over here."

"Air," gasped the little man. "I'm expiring for lack of air."

"Relax and you'll use up less of what we've got left," she advised as Assault escorted him to her.

"Just let me make my peace with my gods and pass away quietly so—"

"How many drinks tonight?"

Forger didn't meet her eyes. "Oh, a few, child."

"Hands. Hold 'em out."

Reluctantly Forger obliged. His gnarled hands fluttered like insects in the wind. "Well, maybe a half dozen. Now I think of it."

"Well, you're still the best gadget man we've got," she said. "So we'll go with you, Forger." She jerked a thumb at the nearest door. "From what we found out in the dark, these damn doors are all jammed."

"So I heard, child."

"You're going to open one of 'em."

"Oh, that's a mighty tough task," protested Forger, shivering. "Especially for a man on the brink of death."

"You'll go over the brink, with a push from me, if you don't quit stalling." She grabbed him by the neck, hustled him to the doorway. "Take a look, study it and then figure out how it can be opened. If it can."

"Any door can be opened, lass." Forger straightened up, rubbed his fingertips together. "All it takes is . . . um . . . time."

Starbuck paused to light a cigar. "How're we doing?"

Apollo's voice replied, "So far three Cylons have hit the battlestar."

"We've taken out a healthy percentage of the others—oops! Here comes another one."

The lieutenant fired his guns.

The Cylon fighter exploded.

"As I was saying," Starbuck said.

"Listen," said Apollo. "I've been in touch with the bridge. Because of those suicide crashes the power's out on much of the starboard side of the battlestar."

"That's where the rec lounge is."

"Yep, and they've got no air coming in."

"They'll die. Robber . . . Roberta and all of them."

"There's a crew trying to get to them."

"Damn it, I ought to be down there."

"We've still got a job to take care of up here," reminded Apollo.

"Then let's finish it up," suggested Starbuck, teeth clamping down on the cigar.

CHAPTER TWENTY-EIGHT

Robber reached back and caught hold of a chair. Sliding it over, she straddled it and continued watching Forger at work.

Using the small tool kit he carried with him, the old man had removed a metal panel from the door. "Here's your trouble right here," he explained over his shoulder, pointing at a tangle of multicolored wires within the door. "Some of these got cooked when—"

"How long to fix?"

"Hard to tell, lass." Frowning, he took another look back at her. "You look a mite peaked."

"Don't worry." She was breathing shallowly, having trouble concentrating on what he was telling her.

Assault crouched on the floor nearby. "What do you think about our chances, Robber?"

"Prophecy isn't my strong suit," she answered. Her voice sounded stranger to her, unfamiliar and faraway.

"You okay?" He moved to her side, rested a hand on her shoulder.

"Matter of fact," she admitted, "I don't feel all that great."

At the other side of the dimly lit room a middle-aged woman began sobbing, short gasping sobs. "Time's run out . . . we'll all die . . ."

"That doesn't help," Robber said in her direction. "Don't give up until . . ."

An unsettling thing happened.

She lost some time.

Not much, she thought. Perhaps only a few microns. But it scared the hell out of her.

She'd been saying something at the sobbing woman, trying to cheer her up and get her to quiet down. Then, with no trace at all of the time in between, Robber was on her knees on the rec lounge floor.

Assault had his powerful arm around her. "C'mon," he was urging, "don't give in."

When she inhaled, her chest hurt. "Don't look so glum," she told him. "I'm a long way from expiring."

Forger was chuckling to himself. "Ah, that's what's wrong," he muttered. "I should've seen that before."

Robber started to ask, "Have you . . ."

She went away again.

But this time she didn't come back.

Colonel Tigh allowed himself a thin smile. "Appears as though," he said, guardedly optimistic, "the worst is over."

Beside him Commander Adama stood studying the scanner screen. "Only two Cylon attackers left," he said, gratified.

"Make that one," said Tigh, pointing as a blip of

light vanished from view. "Correction. None."

Moving nearer his daughter, Commander Adama asked, "What's the situation with the rec lounge?"

"The rescue crew," replied Athena, "is still a corridor away. Getting through the jammed doors is what's slowing them down."

"Colonel," ordered the commander, "get the repair teams to work. We want the power in that area restored as quickly as possible."

"At once," responded Tigh.

"Perhaps we can get the aircirc system functioning in there in time to help," Adama said.

"I don't know," said Athena, "what I'm going to tell poor Starbuck when he gets back."

"You may have good news," said the commander.

Starbuck's cigar was dead.

He let it stay that way.

Once his Viper was safely landed in the docking bay, he got out of the safety gear, popped the cockpit door and jumped clear.

"Hey, Apollo," he called, "have you heard anything?"

Apollo didn't answer until Starbuck caught up with him on the walkway. "They got themselves out of the rec lounge," he said, "and into a corridor where there was still air."

"That's great."

"A rescue crew met them there."

"Terrific. Then I guess . . ." He paused, looking at Apollo. "But that's not a good news face you're wearing."

"Well, old buddy . . ."

Starbuck grabbed his friend's arm. "Don't hold

anything back," he said. "Is something wrong with Robber...with Roberta?"

Apollo gave a slow nod. "She's in the infirmary."

"How serious?"

"They don't know yet."

"Okay." Starbuck clenched his fists, getting control of himself. "Okay. She's not dead, right?"

"No."

"Fine, then there's a chance," said Starbuck. "I'm going to see her now."

"They may not let you into—"

"Oh, yeah, they'll let me," Starbuck assured him. "Because the mood I'm in, I don't think anybody's going to risk trying to stop me."

Whiteness all around her.

Robber took a deep breath and air filled her lungs.

"I'm alive, huh?" she said to nobody in particular.

"That you are, very much so," said the white-clad young medic who was standing beside the white bed she found herself in.

She poked at herself through the white coverlet. "Hey, somebody swiped my clothes."

"Standard procedure," he explained.

"Yeah, but I looked so damn nice in those things."

"You'll get them back."

"How soon?"

"We don't expect you to be here long."

"What's wrong with me?"

"Nothing serious. Basically you passed out from lack of oxygen and—"

"What about Forger?"

"The fellow who opened the door?"

"Good, he did it then?"

"Yes, and everyone got out and to a place where the aircirc system wasn't on the fritz."

Robber nodded to herself, pleased. "That's good news," she said. "But I'm unhappy about passing out. I hope the word on that doesn't get around."

The young medic smiled. "Afraid it already has," he informed her. "Just about everyone knows about how you took charge of the situation, got the fellow to open the door, worked to keep the others calm."

"Sure, I'm some kind of damned hero."

"Well, that's my opinion," he said. "Oh, and I'm now going to violate the rules."

"How?" She eyed him.

"I'm going to allow you a visitor. For a short while anyway," he said. "Then I want you to rest. We have a few more tests to run later on."

"Is this visitor who I think it is?"

"Exactly," said the medic. "Who else but Starbuck could talk his way in here at a time like this?" Crossing to a white door, he opened it. "Come in, Lieutenant. And try to control your usual exuberance." He left the room.

Starbuck made a very subdued entrance and came over to the bedside.

"Hi," he said.

"Hi," she said.

CHAPTER TWENTY-NINE

Starbuck studied himself in his bathroom mirror. "No wonder I'm the idol of millions," he remarked. "Adored throughout the universe and—"

"Spare me," requested Apollo, who was slouched in a comfortable chair.

"I merely state the truth."

"Oh, I wasn't aware that any of what you've been babbling was the truth."

"You have to make an effort to keep up with the latest news." The lieutenant gave his blond hair a final touch with the brush.

"Well, even though it's painful to listen to this," said Apollo, "I am glad to see you're no longer sunk in gloom."

"Nope, I am bubbling over with good feelings." He smoothed a sleeve, patted a crease in his trousers. "After all, we seem to have spooked the Cylons out of this neck of the universe."

"For a while, anyway."

"And that means the colony on Proteus is going to have a chance to get going."

"True."

"And in the days since the attack on the *Galactica* she's been repaired and refurbished," he said, "and everything is shipshape once more."

"And Robber was released from the infirmary."

"That, too," said Starbuck. "But let's remember to call her Roberta."

"Roberta." Apollo watched him in silence for a moment. "You're dining on the Rising Star tonight?"

"I am. Hence all this duding up of myself."

"Can you afford that, good buddy?"

"Interesting that you should ask. Because I have been able to borrow just sufficient funds to finance an evening of—"

"Did you take some kind of commission on that Ambrosa that Assault and the others brought here with them from Proteus?"

Shaking his head, Starbuck pressed a hand to his chest. "I didn't take part in any of the negotiations betwixt Assault and our quartermasters," he said. "Of course, if I hadn't pointed out to Assault that their Ambrosa was so darn valuable, why, they might've left it piled up on the Proteus docks. Right?"

"So you did collect something?"

Starbuck spread his hands wide. "I was given, chum, what is known as an honorarium."

"That's one name for it."

"A nice polite one."

Apollo stretched up out of the chair, shaking his head but grinning. "Well, I hope you don't choke on your dinner this evening."

"Listen, I got interrupted the last time I tried this,"

Starbuck told him, "and sent out on patrol. This time I plan to get all the way through the darn meal."

Robber asked, "Well?"

Starbuck circled the young woman, rubbing thoughtfully on his chin. "It's my considered opinion," he said, "that you look absolutely terrific."

"Hey, I don't want flattery and—"

"A Starbuck never flatters," the lieutenant informed her. "You really do look just fine."

"Ever since they turned me loose from that damn infirmary, I've been sort of uneasy," she said. "Passing out like that . . . well, hell, it shook my confidence. I keep thinking maybe I'm an invalid."

"To me you seem to be in what is known in medical circles as crackerjack shape."

"And my clothes are okay?"

"When I escort you to dinner at the Rising Star, envy will be the emotion all other guys'll feel. The ladies will be visited with jealousy."

"Sure," she said. "The thing I'm worried about . . . this is the first time I . . . you know, that I've been out in public, so to speak. Except for that party the other night."

"And that didn't end up so well." Starbuck crossed to the door. "Even though you proved to be the heroine of the evening."

"C'mon, quit kidding me."

"You know, that's my burden in life," he complained as he opened the door. "I keep telling folks nothing but the truth and they keep accusing me of kidding or boasting."

Smiling, she took his arm. "I guess I'm just not used to somebody like you."

"How could you be? There's nobody else like me in the whole darn universe."

The grey-haired waiter smiled broadly. "One is overjoyed to see you again, Lieutenant," he said, bowing impressively. "And more is delighted at having this opportunity to meet, even in one's humble professional capacity, this admirable young lady. For even here the news of her courageous deed has penetrat—"

"It was Forger opened the damn door," put in Robber. "All I did was tell the nitwit to—"

"Since you're so buoyed up," Starbuck mentioned to the waiter, "you should be able to arrange a private dining room for us."

"You really desire one, sir?" The waiter blinked. "One was of the opinion that, in the light of what took place on the last memorable occasion that you honored us with your—"

"Nevertheless, I'm in the mood to do everything in style tonight," said Starbuck. "So lead on."

"Very well, sir," said the waiter, not moving from the spot where he'd first greeted them. "One does have one room available. However . . ."

Starbuck started to reach into his pocket for a coin. "Maybe this'll—"

"No, no, one isn't angling for an honorarium, sir," the waiter assured him with a quick shake of his head. "One merely wished you to be aware of certain facts, so that there wouldn't be a repetition of what occurred before."

Starbuck frowned. "You don't mean . . . ?"

"Yes, one does. The other young ladies," said the waiter. "The very two you were dining with, or ought one to say attempting to dine with, on that fateful eve.

They happen—even as we speak—to be occupying the dining cubicle next to the one you desire."

"Cassiopea?"

"The same, sir."

"Athena?"

"As well."

"Having dinner?"

"Together, sir."

"That's odd."

"One couldn't help overhearing a portion of their conversation," the waiter told him. "They seem to be drawn together...um...by a mutual...um...how shall one phrase this?...By a shared antipathy for you, Lieutenant."

Starbuck scratched his head. "Roberta, I hope you won't think me a coward," he said to the young woman. "But I don't think we ought to dine in the vicinity of these two ladies."

"I can understand that," she said.

The waiter lowered his voice. "Might one recommend the cafe on the next level, sir? Not as posh, nor as well-staffed, as we are. But it provides many a shadowy corner and intimate nook. It also has the advantage, one hastens to add, of being nowhere near the two young ladies in question."

"That's a terrific suggestion." Taking Robber's hand, Starbuck led her toward the nearest exit from the Rising Star. She asked, "Are you going to explain all this to me sometime?"

"This very night," he promised. "And probably at great length."